God, he craved her more than he'd ever craved anyone.

Creed would have liked to launch himself across the room, and take Yvonne to that heaven known only to vampires and their victims. But he certainly wouldn't do it to a woman who had turned to him for protection.

If this was a test, he teetered on the edge of failing it miserably.

In desperation, he went into his bedroom and locked himself safely within. In here her smell would dissipate. In here he could no longer hear her heartbeat.

Rarely did he retire before dawn, but this night he could do nothing else. He could not afford to think about the delicious morsel lying on his couch.

Trusting him.

Dear Reader,

Another journey into THE CLAIMING was irresistible to me. The notion that vampires themselves can become so enthralled that it's a matter of life and death for them gave rise to some of the events in this book.

Vampires have a lot of powers, and few weaknesses other than the sun. I skipped the part about the stake to the heart because that's never appealed to me, but I felt there should be another weakness vampires are prey to, and thus The Claiming.

As you will find in these pages, The Claiming is love raised to the nth degree. No vampire wants it to happen, knowing full well its risks.

In *Claimed by a Vampire*, I also got to deal with a vampire who once had a wife and children but had to give them up because he had become a threat to them. He never wanted to love again because he had lost so much. Instead he finds himself drawn to a woman, a novelist, who needs his protection and who is also reluctant to become involved.

Each is wounded, one by love too good, and one by love too bad. And the bad love is the one that comes back to haunt them.

Enjoy!

Rachel

CLAIMED BY A VAMPIRE

RACHEL LEE

All the characters in this book have no existence outside the imagination of the author, and have no relation whatsoever to anyone bearing the same name or names. They are not even distantly inspired by any individual known or unknown to the author, and all the incidents are pure invention.

First published in Great Britain 2012
by Mills & Boon, an imprint of Harlequin (UK) Limited,
Eton House, 18-24 Paradise Road, Richmond, Surrey TW9 1SR

ISBN: 978 0 263 89598 8
ebook ISBN: 978 1 408 97481 0

089-0512

Harlequin (UK) policy is to use papers that are natural, renewable and recyclable products and made from wood grown in sustainable forests. The logging and manufacturing processes conform to the legal environmental regulations of the country of origin.

Printed and bound in Spain
by Blackprint CPI, Barcelona

Rachel Lee was hooked on writing by the age of twelve, and practiced her craft as she moved from place to place all over the United States. This *New York Times* bestselling author now resides in Florida and has the joy of writing full-time.

Chapter 1

Creed Preston sat in the outer office of Messenger Investigations, amusing himself by watching the swirl and flow around him. Jude Messenger had been his friend for years, but only recently had he become comfortable enough to spend a lot of time in Jude's office, surrounded by mortals like Terri, Chloe and Garner.

It was a vampire thing. He and Jude had cemented a friendship that crossed the final barriers of territoriality that most of their kind felt, often to an extreme degree, when Jude had risked his life to eliminate the evil that had nearly killed Creed's great-granddaughter.

But spending much time in the company of mortals could still be painful, because they smelled so damned tempting. As the years passed, however, his self-control became easier, and over the past months since Jude had mated with a mortal, Terri, he'd learned he could enjoy their company and control his hunger well enough.

Terri was absent this evening. As an assistant medical examiner, she often had to go out at night to crime scenes. Chloe sat at her desk, wearing her signature punk-cum-stripper getup, her hair dyed black and worn in spikes. She topped the whole image off with enough black eye makeup to keep a cosmetics company in business, and bright red lipstick.

Across from her sat Garner, a gifted demon hunter of about twenty-five, blond and blue-eyed, and casually elegant in a scruffy sort of way. The two of them often argued like siblings.

Creed enjoyed listening to their spats. Once, long ago, he'd had children, and he'd been forced to watch from a distance as they grew old and died. When Chloe and Garner got going, he inevitably grinned and watched the show.

Jude, however, had no such background with kids, and had a great deal less patience.

"Will you two cut it out?" he called from his inner office. "I'm trying to think."

Both Chloe and Garner fell silent, but continued to shoot fiery looks at one another.

Sitting here, Creed felt more "normal" than he had since his change. Which was probably why he was spending more and more time in this office, as his own job allowed.

He put a hand over his mouth to hide a smile and continued to watch the dagger-staring contest. As usual, Garner wanted to plunge headlong into something dangerous without even grasping how dangerous it was, and Chloe displayed enough common sense to be twice her twenty-five years. And keeping quiet was obviously stressing their self-control.

Jude, his fellow vampire, appeared in the door of his office. As always, he was dressed in a perfectly tailored black silk shirt and slacks. Most vampires preferred black because it helped them blend with the shadows. Creed himself wore black slacks and a black turtleneck sweater. He didn't share Jude's taste for finer clothes.

Jude was slightly above average height, three inches shorter than Creed, and right now his eyes, golden from recent feeding, were not quite golden enough. He was irritated or disturbed.

Jude looked at Chloe and Garner. "Have you two concocted a plan for how we're going to deal with this?"

Neither answered him.

"I thought not," Jude said, sarcasm edging his tone. "All that arguing and no plan. Why doesn't that surprise me?"

"Because you know us," Chloe said with a toss of her head. "Look, boss, you ought to just let Garner go do what he wants. Then we won't have to deal with him anymore."

"Hey!" said Garner. "How do you know I'm not right?"

"Because *you* suggested it?" Chloe arched one brow.

Garner glared.

"Enough," Jude said quietly. That one word quelled them both.

Jude looked at Creed. "I need to go keep an eye on Terri. You want to come?"

"Because of this *thing?*"

Jude nodded. "She was a doorway last time. She might still be. I don't know."

Creed understood. Jude had offered to die permanently to save them all from the thing that had nearly killed Creed's great-granddaughter, that had attacked Terri, as well. He also understood that no matter how many cops surrounded Terri, none of them would be able to protect her from that kind of threat.

He rose. "Sure."

He didn't have to ask Jude how they would find her. Jude and Terri's relationship was more than a simple mating; it was a claiming. No matter where Terri went now, Jude would be able to find her. And if anything happened to Terri, Jude would probably tear the planet apart before he killed himself.

It was the way of vampires. And the reason most of them tried to avoid a claiming at all costs: inevitably, if something went wrong, death and destruction would result.

But apparently, to judge by the way Jude had claimed Terri despite all the warnings he'd given Creed about it over the years, claiming wasn't always a choice.

They left the car because they had no need for it. Jude carried the tools of his trade in the pockets of a long leather coat: crucifix, the ritual for exorcism and plenty of holy water. Creed felt a bit uncomfortable with that, but some of his perspectives were undergoing radical changes because of his association with Jude.

They slipped from shadow to shadow too fast for human eyes to see. The most any mortal could have noticed would have been the breeze of their passage.

The city was quieting down though, falling into its late slumber at last, so they didn't encounter many people.

Each one, though, had a particular, tempting aroma. It was, Creed sometimes thought wryly, like slipping through an aromatic deli but never tasting a single, delicious morsel. With time it got easier, though never easy.

He had vowed a long time ago never to become again that ravenous monster he'd been during the weeks and months after his change. If he ever felt weak, his conscience summoned up a whole banquet of ugly images to remind him of what he had done.

Though sometimes he wondered why he bothered. Humans were so good at doing *themselves* in, it often felt pointless for him to suppress his own urges, his own hunger.

Jude took them directly to the crime scene. His instincts had guided him to Terri as surely as a homing beacon. Together they mounted a nearby building and watched from the roof. Periodically, Jude lifted his head and sniffed the air to make sure there was nothing unusual about.

From above, both preternatural sight and preternatural hearing allowed Creed to know everything that was going on. Most of it was dull, detail work, and he hardly paid attention. He didn't really care about the ordinary details of an ordinary murder. Finally, bored, he tuned it out and looked up at the stars.

Despite the city lights, he could see thousands of them, if not millions, thanks to his vision. Sparkling in all the colors of the rainbow and more, they seemed to set the sky ablaze. He loved moonless nights because he could see so many more stars.

For him the night was not leached of color, but instead flooded with it. Things he had never been able to see as a human now filled his eyes with pleasure. Sounds and scents brought him stories of the night that he would never have noticed before.

No, it was not all bad.

"Creed?"

He dragged his gaze from the heavens to look at Jude. "What?"

"Do you smell it?"

Creed drew the night into his lungs, smelling it and tasting it. He paused, then exhaled slowly. "There's something faint. Something *off*."

"It was here. Gone now, but it was here."

At once Creed's interest in the goings-on below him returned. He focused on the little hive of human activity, listening and watching.

"Do you think it caused this?" he asked Jude.

"I don't know. I'll find out more from Terri. For now though, it's enough to know it was here."

"And good reason to stick around Terri until she's home."

"Yeah. Thanks, Creed."

"I don't know how much good I'll be if needed." Then Creed paused. "So, okay, maybe you need to teach me how to deal with this stuff."

"It would be helpful."

Creed had never wanted to enter the world where Jude existed, fighting demons and other unseen threats. It had always seemed to him to be a dangerous path full of hidden pitfalls, and he was at heart still the Harvard professor he'd been before his own change. But after what had happened to his great-granddaughter, his opinion had rapidly shifted. Now he'd just offered to jump in with both feet.

Surprising himself, he grinned into the night. Apparently he'd made the decision without realizing it.

He drew another lungful of the night. The abnormal scent was already cataloged in a part of his brain that would never forget it. He would know it again the instant he encountered it anywhere. So he sniffed, checking for it, making sure it didn't strengthen. For now that was all he could do.

"It doesn't seem to be coming back," Jude

remarked presently, as the team below them began to pack up, as the body was loaded into a morgue van. "Why don't you run back to the office, or home if you prefer. I'll just follow Terri to the morgue to make sure it's not in the vicinity. Then I'll get back to the office."

"What if you find it? I should come, too."

Jude smiled without humor. "I don't want to challenge it tonight unless I have no choice. I'm just keeping an eye out."

"Call me if you need me." Then Creed straightened and blended away into the night like a shadow.

Being a vampire *did* have its advantages.

Since it was still several hours before dawn, Creed chose to head back to Jude's office. He didn't feel like working tonight, and Chloe and Garner often provided amusement.

He now had his own key card and code to enter, so he got no warning at all when he walked down the darkened hallway and opened the door to Jude's office. Inside were not only Chloe and Garner, but another young woman, maybe thirty.

And the minute he stepped through the door, her scent hit him like a speeding train. Instant hunger, almost overwhelming, slammed him, followed by a near-intoxication. He froze, never having experienced such a strong reaction before, and fought for his self-control. No morsel had ever smelled so good to him.

"Hi, Creed," Chloe said.

He couldn't even answer her. Instead he stared at the young woman who sat beside Chloe's desk. Blonde, her hair falling loose from a chignon as if the wind had ripped at her. Wearing a white wool dress that hinted at a lovely figure. Her face might have been painted by an artist trying to capture the beauty of an angel, her eyes a green so bright they almost seemed to glow.

But it was her scent that punched him, held him rigid in the hell between hunger and self-control.

"Creed?" Chloe said.

With an extreme effort, he dragged his gaze from the woman and looked at Chloe. "Hi," he managed.

"This is Yvonne Depuis. She's here to see Jude. Do you know when he'll be back?"

"I'm not sure. He wanted to make sure Terri made it safely back to the morgue."

"Morgue?" Yvonne Depuis's eyes widened.

"Terri is a medical examiner," Chloe said swiftly. "She's been out at a crime scene."

"Who is Terri?"

"Jude's…wife," Chloe answered, shading the truth a bit.

"Oh." Yvonne tried a smile. The way the corners of her mouth trembled called to Creed. He had to force himself to cross the room and sit on the couch as if nothing at all was happening, certainly not the momentous response inside himself.

"This is silly," Yvonne said to Chloe. "Everyone's going to laugh at me."

"Honey," Chloe said, "around here we don't laugh at anything except Garner."

From his corner of the room, Garner snorted.

"Okay, then you'll think I'm nuts."

"We don't do that, either," Chloe said, sending a significant look to Creed. Just as he wondered what she meant, she added, "Do we, Creed?"

"Um, no." From Chloe's look he could tell he was required to elaborate, so he said, "At least not since my…relative was attacked by a demon, I certainly don't laugh."

Yvonne turned in her chair and looked at him. "Really?"

"Really," he answered grimly, and wished she'd look away because, well, he was getting perilously close to losing the battle with his natural instincts.

What the hell was wrong with him? Maybe he should just bail now and go home to work. It would be the safer alternative. But as he stared at the blonde something else struck him.

"Do I know you?"

He was horrified to see her blush faintly, because that rising blood in her cheeks called to him like water in a desert.

"I, uh, I saw you once," she admitted. "You were on your way out of the building as I was walking up. I think that was when I was thinking about buying the condo there."

Now he remembered. The briefest moments in passing as he left his building, moving as fast as possible while pretending to be human, to avoid noticing anyone, to avoid the kind of neighborly contact that could create problems. He could easily have missed her scent, if the wind was right and he was going the other way. "Did you buy it?"

"Yes." She furrowed her brow a bit. "Don't you own one of the penthouses?"

Something in him stilled. She had troubled to find out where he lived, which meant her interest was more than passing. He needed to keep an eye on her. "Yes," he said after a moment. "The topmost."

She nodded. "Nice to meet you, neighbor." Then she turned back to Chloe.

He wasn't sure this was nice at all, not when he considered how hard he worked to make certain his neighbors just plain didn't notice him.

He had put out the cover story that he was a reclusive intellectual with a medical problem who worked odd hours on papers for an international relations think tank, all of which was true except for the recluse part. Of course, being a vampire could be considered a medical problem.

He made sure to be seen leaving by way of the lobby once in a while, and coming back the same way so questions wouldn't be asked, he had food delivered which he then carted out in smaller quantities to a food bank, and his blood deliveries sailed in safely under the banner of his "medical problem."

But why had she asked about him, based on one small glimpse of him leaving the building?

He stared at her back and wished Jude would hurry up. He had questions now about this woman, and they were questions he could not ask. But Jude could, without making her suspicious.

The phone rang and Chloe answered. "Hi, Jude! When will you be back? You've got a client waiting. Okay. I'll tell her."

Chloe hung up and smiled at Yvonne. "He says fifteen minutes, max."

Creed wished he could see more than the back of Yvonne's head. Could feel more than uneasiness and a strong desire to pounce. Her aroma kept wafting his way, and only curiosity kept him from going home now to get out of the range of temptation.

And only self-restraint kept him glued to the couch. Finally, desperate, he announced, "I need some air," and walked out. He waited outside on the quieting night street in the cold autumn air, impervious to the temperature.

And then Jude emerged from the shadows.

Creed had heard his approach, though no mortal ever would have.

"What's up?" Jude asked.

"Your new client."

Jude came to stand beside him. "What?"

"She lives in my building, just moved there."

"Okay."

"And she knows where I live even though she claims to have seen me only once."

"That made you suspicious."

It wasn't a question, which Creed appreciated. "You know the profile I keep. Of course it made me suspicious. She shouldn't have noticed me enough to be curious. All I did was pass her quickly on my way out one night."

"Well, some humans do feel an instinctive fascination."

"Maybe. But then she turns up at your office."

Jude nodded. "Consider me on guard. Maybe you should go home."

"I'm curious. But her scent…"

Jude suddenly laughed. "Okay. I understand that one. Terri's scent about drove me nuts. Can you handle it long enough to satisfy your curiosity?"

"I'll have to. If you see her in confidence, you can't tell me a damn thing."

"Then come on. Let's go get our answers."

"But not for long. Crap. Now I'm blowing my cover as a medically troubled recluse."

"We can take care of that, too. But first let's find out what's going on."

Creed followed him inside, his step heavier than usual.

Inside, Jude shook hands with Yvonne Depuis and invited her into his inner office. Sometimes Creed thought Jude had been born suave, but he'd also seen Jude's other side—impatient and occasionally cranky. On leaden feet, he went into Jude's office with them, and took a chair as far away from Yvonne as space allowed.

"Mr. Preston," Jude explained to Yvonne, "consults with me as his health allows, so I'm sure you don't mind if he stays with us while we discuss your problem."

Good going, Jude, Creed thought.

Yvonne shot another glance at Creed and again colored. "No, of course not. Might as well have the entire world think I'm crazy."

"We don't often think that around here,"

Jude said soothingly. He pulled a piece of paper in front of him and picked up a pen. "What brought you to Messenger Investigations?"

"A friend of mine is on the police force. She said you have a reputation for dealing with weird stuff."

Jude smiled. "So we do. Who recommended us? I like to thank people for referrals."

"Detective Matthews."

"Ah, Pat. A very nice lady."

"She taught a criminology course I took a number of years ago and we became friends."

"You're in the police, too?"

Yvonne shook her head. "Not my cup of tea. I was just curious about law enforcement. I'm a writer. I'm curious about a lot of things."

Jude nodded, scribbling something. "And the problem that brought you to us?"

Yvonne bit her lower lip. Creed inevitably thought about how he'd like to bite it for her. He had to close his eyes for a moment.

"It's so hard to explain."

"But you managed to tell Pat about it."

A tremulous sigh escaped her and she managed another nod. "Okay. I moved into my condo about a week ago. And since I did, well, it's hard to explain. I've never felt like this before. But I feel continually watched. Never alone. Every single minute I'm there. And then some things got moved around and I *know* I didn't move them."

"So you think someone may be getting in?"

"I don't know. I mean that feeling of being watched… If someone was there, I'd know it. The condo's not big enough for someone to really hide for long. But no one's ever there. Frankly, I don't even want to be alone in my own home, and it's only been a week. The feeling is getting stronger. At first I thought it was just being in a new place, but if that was the case, it would be wearing off, wouldn't it? And things being moved…" She shook her head and released a heavy sigh. "I can't afford to move out now. I just bought the place. So I have to find out what's wrong."

"I agree," Jude said. "Whatever it is that's making you feel this way, we need to get to the bottom of it."

"So you don't think I'm just crazy?"

"Not likely. I think Creed will concur, when one feels watched, there's usually someone watching."

Creed cleared his throat. "Studies would seem to bear that out."

"God." Yvonne shuddered. "How could that be?" Then she appeared to have a thought. "Maybe it's that creep of an ex-boyfriend of mine. Maybe he did something to my computer. He could be watching me day and night." She scowled. "I wouldn't put it past him, considering all the weird things he seems to get into. Stalking me? Yes, he'd be capable of it."

"We'll check it out along with other possibilities," Jude said. "I want to examine your apartment very closely. I'll need to gather some equipment first, though. When would be a good time?"

"Any time," she said vehemently. "Now, tomorrow, I don't care when. I work at home. Or I do when I'm not creeped out. Just tell me when."

"Tomorrow night," Jude said. "And I'm going to have Creed here accompany you home and check out your apartment before he goes to his own."

Creed found it almost impossible to maintain a straight face. Alone with that woman in her apartment? Had Jude just lost his mind? But

Jude's expression revealed nothing. Talk about the ultimate test of self-control.

"Thank you," Yvonne said, looking at him. "I'd be so grateful."

Like hell she would, he thought grimly. Whatever or whoever might be watching her, it probably wasn't nearly as big a threat to her as a vampire who craved her blood.

Namely Creed.

Chapter 2

Yvonne was acutely aware of Creed following her in his big black SUV as she drove back home. But then she'd been acutely aware of him since first she'd seen him, that day she decided to buy the condo. Maybe she had even made the decision because of him.

God, wasn't she too old for a crush? Evidently not, because one sight of Creed Preston had engraved him indelibly in her mind. He was handsome, with an elegant build. He moved like an athlete, and the gold color of his eyes was striking. Like a tiger's eyes, she thought.

And something about him struck her as dangerous, but not in a bad way. How weird was that? Maybe it was his tiger's eyes.

But not even for long could she distract herself with thoughts of a silly schoolgirl crush, and how ridiculous that was in a woman of thirty-two. She was heading home again, heading to that place she called home anyway, a place that not even for one instant seemed welcoming anymore. In one short week she had come to wish that she'd noticed that feeling of being watched *before* she had bought the place. Because now all she wanted was to get out of it. Fast.

She pulled into her slot in the building's parking garage and waited while Creed pulled into his. The penthouse slots were nearer the elevator, hardly surprising. When he climbed out, she felt again his extraordinary impact and wondered why she responded that way.

His smile was nice, too, even if it looked a bit forced. He used his own key to open the elevator then waved her in ahead of him. He seemed to her to hesitate, but only for a split second, before entering the car with her. She must have imagined it.

"Which floor?" he asked, reaching for the buttons.

"Twenty-fourth."

He punched the button, then leaned back against the far wall, not looking at her. Indeed, he almost seemed to hold his breath.

Was she that repulsive to him? She knew she looked rather mousy, in fact it was an appearance she mostly cultivated in order to be left alone, but she didn't think she stank. Had nervousness outworn her deodorant or something?

Irritated, she glanced away from him and watched the floors tick by. The ride seemed unusually long, and when finally the doors opened, she stepped out quickly and turned to face him.

"Look," she said, her tone a little sharp, "I don't want to inconvenience you any more. I'll just deal with it tonight and wait for Mr. Messenger tomorrow."

He straightened, pulling away from the car wall, and held out an arm so the elevator doors wouldn't close. "I'm sorry?"

"Well, I can tell you'd rather be elsewhere. Clearly something about me repels you."

Both his brows lifted. Then he astonished her with a laugh. "You've got that exactly backward."

"What?" Now she felt confused.

"Nothing about you repels me," he said flatly. "Quite the contrary. And I insist on checking out your apartment. Jude wants me to, I'm concerned about what you're feeling, and if possible, I'd like to experience it, too. Unless you really *do* want to go back there by yourself tonight?"

Her jaw dropped a little. Had she totally misread him? His body language had definitely made her feel that he wanted to be away from her. But he'd told her the exact opposite was true. What was she to believe?

Finally, she managed a shrug and let him follow her to her door. Pat had recommended Jude Messenger, and Jude had vouched for Creed, so there was absolutely no reason on earth to suspect this man of anything except a desire to help her.

She must be too stressed, must be reading things wrong. Certainly she was short on sleep.

She swiped the key card at her door and pushed it open.

And the minute she stepped inside she felt it. Only now it was stronger than the sense of being watched. It was as if something dark loomed over her, threatening her. "Oh, God," she whispered.

"Stay here," Creed said. "Keep the door open." He slipped past her into her condo.

As if she could have moved anyway. The sense of a presence overwhelmed her. The air thickened with menace, and it was stronger than she'd ever felt it before. She would not, could not, walk farther inside.

She waited with a hammering heart, straining to hear, but hearing nothing. Then, almost too quickly to be believed, Creed reappeared.

"Nothing?" she asked, knowing damn well it was *something*.

"I wouldn't say that." He pulled his cell phone from a belt clip and pressed a button. "Jude? That thing? It's been here. Recently. Yes, I can smell it."

"What thing?" Yvonne asked, barely able to whisper the words because her heart was pounding so hard she couldn't seem to get enough air.

Creed didn't answer her. "Okay," he said,

then put away his phone. When he did, he looked at her.

"Can you handle a few more minutes?"

"Why?"

"Because I want to search your apartment."

A shudder ripped through her. "For what? You'd have seen anyone who was there."

"I need to look for some other stuff. And that brings me to your options."

"What options? I don't have any." Some part of her hated the weakness and fear she heard in her own voice.

"You can stay at a hotel tonight, or you can stay at my place. I have a decent couch you can use. But I have to warn you, if you stay with me."

"Warn me about what?" She was having trouble absorbing all this. What had he sensed? She needed answers. Her brain was still stumbling over the fact that he had smelled something, something he referred to as *that thing.* How could she decide what she should do tonight when she had no idea what she faced?

"I'm…ill," he said. "My skin reacts badly to bright light. I won't bore you with the medical stuff, but suffice it to say that at dawn I lock myself in my bedroom and I don't come out again until dusk. I can't. So if you stay with me, I can offer protection only for a few hours. After that, you can stay as long as you like but don't come back here."

She nodded slowly, feeling punched, her thoughts scrambling. She didn't want to accept favors from Creed Preston—or anyone for that matter—but she couldn't bear the thought of being alone given what she was feeling right now. What if this thing, whatever it was, could follow her?

Her mind stuttered to a halt, then focused on the one certainty in her life, the one thing she loved beyond all else. Her thoughts seized on it as an anchor, stilling. "Can I at least have my laptop? So I can work?"

"I'll get it. Anything else?"

She thought of nightclothes, a change of clothing. Did she want him pawing through her things? But did she want to be stuck in what she was wearing forever? "I need to come in. I need a change of clothes." She hated that she could hear fear and reluctance in her own voice. This was her own condo, for Pete's sake. She couldn't even begin to sort through the welter of emotions that reminder caused her. Afraid to go into her own home? Afraid to spend just a few minutes packing? But her feet felt glued to the floor.

He hesitated. “No,” he said finally. “No. I’ll get them. Trust me, I was married once, and had daughters, and I’ll treat your things with respect. And I won’t see anything I haven’t seen before.”

The thought of walking farther into that miasma, into that threatening heaviness, forced her answer. “There’s a suitcase on the shelf in the closet.”

He nodded. “Step outside. You’ll feel better.”

She followed his direction and discovered that indeed, just a few steps away from her door, she felt better. Now how was that possible? The question was almost enough to make her walk back into her apartment. Almost.

But the memory of the feeling that had slapped her the instant she crossed the threshold proved stronger than any desire to check it out. She knew she hadn’t imagined it. Her imagination ran almost entirely to the books she wrote, and rarely affected what she considered to be an otherwise pragmatic view of life.

At least she hoped it was. She hoped the fantasies she spun for her readers weren't beginning to affect her brain.

No, of course they weren't. For heaven's sake, she knew the difference between her imagination and reality. The two only met on the pages on her computer screen.

Suddenly from within her condo, she heard a bang. Instantly she forgot everything else and started back in. One step. Two steps. Then she froze as a blackness seemed to wrap oily tendrils in her brain. No. No!

She tried to back up, but couldn't. It was as if some force tried to drag her forward, deeper within her condo, away from the relative safety of the hall.

And that noise. Something not quite curiosity, something almost like compulsion, wanted to drag her toward it. Feeling almost like a stranger within her own head, she sought the only thing she could to break the spell or whatever it was. She called out, "Creed? What happened?"

Her voice sounded odd, as if it had emerged

from the depths of the ocean. But that was impossible. Her ears hummed. Maybe the loud noise had dulled her hearing for a few seconds. That had to be it.

"Something fell." He sounded far away, as if calling to her from the bottom of a well. "It's fine."

Then, released by whatever had tried to seize her, she backed quickly into the hallway. What the hell was going on? What had she just felt? The only comparison she could come up with was being hypnotized, and she wasn't even sure about that.

Creed emerged from her condo a few minutes later carrying her laptop in its case with all her peripherals, and her suitcase, along with a manila envelope. Apparently he thought of everything.

"If I missed something, you can tell me after we get to my place and I can come back for it."

"Thank you," she said. "I can't tell you how much I appreciate this. Are you sure I won't be a problem?" What was she doing? She ought to go to a hotel, take care of herself. Could she seriously be proposing to burden someone else?

But right now she was more terrified of being alone. Especially after what she had just felt.

"Hardly," he said with a shrug.

"What fell?" she asked as they waited for the elevator.

"A pewter plate. It's fine."

She knew exactly the plate he meant. "There's no way that fell!"

"Okay, it flew at me."

She opened her mouth to tell him to quit kidding when she read his expression. He wasn't kidding. "Oh, my God," she breathed.

He shrugged. "I guess it didn't like me being there."

"*What* didn't like you being there? Creed, for heaven's sake! Are you joshing me? Did it really fly at you?"

"Heaven has nothing to do with this. It flew at me. And that's another reason you're not going back to that place."

"Are you okay?"

"Minor bruise. I'm fine. But I can't promise *you* will be if you go back there."

She felt almost dazed, trying to grasp that that heavy plate could have flown at him, but despite her distraction and confusion she noticed he didn't hesitate to enter the elevator car with her this time. So maybe she had indeed misread him earlier.

But even that couldn't keep her attention now. Considering what she had felt when she entered her condo this time, it was all too easy to believe in flying plates. For the first time she was *truly* grateful that she could stay with him that night. Whatever was going on in her place had just magnified to truly scary proportions, and even a hotel room didn't sound like a safe place right now.

His condo took her breath away. Two long walls of glass gave an eagle's eye view of the night city. The living area was entirely open, punctuated only by a bar that divided the kitchen from the rest. And it was full of color, rich colors and textures that made it seem almost jewel-like but not at all garish.

"This is beautiful!" she exclaimed.

"Glad you like it. When you live most of your life at night, color is essential."

"That must be hard for you."

She noted he didn't answer directly. Most likely, she decided, he didn't care to discuss his problem. Most certainly not with someone he'd just met.

His sidestep was almost seamless. "Do you want to work tonight? I can clear a space on my desk." He gestured to a table that held a computer in front of one of the windows.

"Not tonight. I couldn't possibly concentrate. What do you do?"

"I'm a consultant for a foreign relations think tank."

She looked at him again. "That's impressive." And it was. But he seemed to shrug it away.

"Before I got sick, I taught at Harvard," he answered. "I'm glad I was able to find an alternative that fits within my limitations."

She nodded, sweeping her gaze over the room again. "You certainly have a good eye. I can only dream of making my place look half this good."

"Why do you say that?"

"Because I'm not much of a visual person. I mean, I can see something and know I like it, but putting it together with other things to get an effect like this is beyond me." She wrinkled her nose. "I'm more the verbal type."

"That's what they make decorators for." But he was smiling. "Let me show you where everything is."

The penthouse contained every luxury. There was a bath off to one side, sumptuous in its trappings, with a whirlpool tub and a shower both. Fluffy towels that looked brand-new hung from the racks.

"I never use this," he said. "I have my own off the master bedroom. I have a second bedroom, but I never got around to furnishing it, which is why I have to offer you the couch."

"The couch is fine, really. It looks comfortable."

"I'll get the sheets and blankets for you."

"Wait," she said as he turned away. He paused to look at her, and she felt a frisson of excitement as his golden gaze settled on her. God, he had an intense stare. And his nostrils flared just a bit, as if he were testing the scents in the air.

"Yes?"

"What exactly did you sense in my apartment? What *thing* were you referring to?"

This time there was no way to mistake his hesitation. "You'd need to ask Jude that, honestly. But you know he deals in the unusual. The stuff that most people don't begin to want to deal with."

"The paranormal."

"I guess that's a fair word. Well, there's something he's looking for right now. And I smelled it in your condo."

"*Smelled* it?"

He nodded. "Think back. I know you were overwhelmed by what you felt, but you probably smelled it, too. It wasn't exactly faint."

Now she hesitated, thinking back, feeling an icy prickle along her spine. Had she smelled something? She couldn't be sure. "All I was aware of was this…this sense of something there, a thickening of the air, a feeling of menace. God, that sounds crazy."

"Not to me, it doesn't." His mouth drew into a grim line. "There are forces we don't believe in until we meet them face-to-face, Yvonne. I've met a few of them. I believe."

Before she could answer, he turned again. "I'll make up your bed for you, then I need to work a bit. Most people don't have enough hours in a day. I never have enough in a night."

She watched him disappear down the hall,

and was abruptly struck by what he had told her about his illness. Imagine never being able to see the day again. Imagine living in a world where light was a threat.

And she thought she had problems? But she couldn't help shuddering again.

She changed in the bathroom, touched that he had chosen her one pair of modest pajamas rather than one of the more sensual garments she wore to bed just because they made her feel feminine. He'd even packed her slippers and robe.

Stepping back out into the living room, she found the couch transformed into a bed, and Creed was over at his desk, a distance away given the huge size of this room, working only by the light from his computer screen. The only other light was a dim lamp on the side table at the end of the couch where he'd placed a couple of pillows. Once she switched off that light, the room would be in near-darkness, dappled by the city lights that seemed far away for the most part. Dark enough for sleep.

But instead of heading straight toward the bed, she stopped instead to look at the floor-to-ceiling bookshelves that framed the entry door, covering nearly the entire wall. They were jammed with nonfiction, some of the books looking as if they were a century or more old. Not a work of fiction among them that she could tell.

Then she came upon a section of classics, from Twain to Hawthorne, to Swift. Plays by Shakespeare, Ibsen and others. And all bore the signs of having been handled often.

She wondered if he was an intellectual snob, then decided that wouldn't be a fair assessment to make, especially when he'd been so kind to her.

"Do you need something to read?"

His voice was unexpected and startled her. She turned from his bookshelves to find he had swiveled his desk chair and was looking at her.

"Sorry, I was just curious. Few people these days decorate their walls with books."

He laughed quietly. "Some still do. Most of that is references I need for my work. I'm especially fond of books, and I have a passion for old books. But if you'd prefer something of more recent vintage, I do have some novels lying around. I just don't tend to keep them.

I find they're welcome donations at nursing homes."

So he didn't stick to the classics. That relieved her a bit, given that she wrote popular fiction. She hated people who looked down on her for that, and sometimes reminded them that Dickens was a hack who wrote serials for newspapers, and that Tolstoy had been paid by the word, hence his lengthy volumes. Apparently she wouldn't need that defense here.

"Thanks, but I was just curious. And I guess I'm edgy."

"Understandable. Frankly, I'm not sure how you managed to stand a whole week in that apartment."

She wandered closer, feeling inexplicably drawn to him. Only when she saw him tense a bit did she stop. Was there something wrong with her?

"It got worse," she said, forcing herself to ignore an unreasoning sense of rejection. "It was awful tonight, the worst ever. When I first moved in I was able to brush the feeling off, but over the week it just kept getting stronger."

"I'm glad you didn't come home alone tonight. I'd hate to think of you forcing yourself to walk in there because it was all you could do."

"I'm not sure I could have." She found an upholstered chair at what she thought might be a safe distance from him, and sat. "It felt like a gut punch tonight. But you said it wasn't still there. To Jude, when you called him."

"But it had been there recently enough to leave its stench and fingerprints everywhere. And apparently it came back long enough to evince disapproval of my presence."

"But what *is* it?"

"Jude will have to explain. I'm a relative newcomer to all of this. He has the experience and knowledge."

"But you said you've seen things, and now you believe."

His eyes seemed to darken, and she wondered if it was some trick of the dim lighting, because for a moment they looked almost black.

"I've seen things," he agreed. "But not *this* thing. I don't know anything about it except it has Jude concerned."

"So he'll tell me tomorrow?"

"Tomorrow night."

She felt an unreasoning chill again. "Why night?"

"He suffers from the same problem that I do. So he works only at night."

"Are you related?"

He shook his head. "Friends. Drawn together by a common experience."

That made sense, so she let it go. "I'm sorry, I'm interrupting your work. I should just try to sleep."

"I have surprisingly little interest in work tonight." He smiled. "Events can be distracting."

"I've gotten very little writing done this week," she admitted. "It's hard to work when you feel someone is looking over your shoulder."

Which, she realized with sudden embarrassment, was exactly what she was doing to him. Basically looking over his shoulder. But as she tried to find a believable reason to go lie on the couch and pretend to sleep when she felt wound as tightly as a spring, he rose.

"Would you like coffee or tea?" he asked.

"Or something to eat? I must have something lying around."

"I'd love coffee if you don't mind."

"I don't mind in the least." He walked into the kitchen and pulled a coffeepot out of the cupboard.

He kept his coffeepot in the cupboard? Then he must not drink it often. Everyone she knew kept it in easy reach on the counter. So maybe he was a tea kind of guy.

But he made no tea, and when he returned to the living room, he did so with a coffee service that held only one cup. He politely poured her coffee then let her add what she wanted. "I'm sorry, I have no cream or milk, but I do have sugar."

"Black is fine, thanks." Ignoring her desire for a little milk in the coffee, she held the cup in her hands and sipped. "You keep your apartment cold," she remarked. The contrast between her cold hands and the hot cup caused her to notice.

"Oh. I forgot to turn the heat on." He at once went to the wall and adjusted the thermostat. "Sorry, I don't notice the chill much. You should have said something sooner."

"I just noticed."

Which was true. But at the same time she found herself wondering what other oddities he had. Most people by this time in the autumn left their heat on all the time.

He was a strange bird indeed, she thought staring down into her cup. Handsome and strange, and the combination intrigued her. Drew her.

She'd never felt particularly drawn to ordinary people. People with quirks, however, were a different matter, and the quirkier the better. That tendency occasionally caused her trouble but she never seemed to learn her lesson.

"You must hate the summer," she blurted. Stealing a look at him, she saw he had raised one eyebrow.

"Why?" he asked.

"Because the days are longer."

"Ah. Well, yes, it means my nights are shorter."

"Does it ever make you crazy, not being able to tolerate the light?"

One corner of his mouth lifted. "Once it did. One adapts, you know. There's quite a bit of beauty in the night."

"I'm a bit of a night owl, myself. But I do like a daily dose of sun." She wondered if the wife and daughters he had mentioned had left him because of his illness, but caught herself before incaution released the question. None of her business. Sheesh, sometimes she forgot how to interact with people because she chose to spend so much time alone in her own little world.

Although he had not in any way indicated it, Yvonne felt she had intruded too much into his life. First by needing to sleep in his living room, and then by engaging him in a conversation when, regardless of what he said, he had clearly intended to work.

She put her cup on the tray. "Thanks for the coffee. I guess I'm getting sleepy after all."

He rose when she did, a gentlemanly courtesy she had thought long dead. As soon as she slipped between the covers on the sofa, she heard him return to his desk. Moments later the quiet tapping of keys filled the room.

She forced herself to close her eyes and pretend to sleep. To avoid thinking about that awful feeling in her apartment.

And the easiest device for avoiding the awful

was to think about an intriguing topic: Creed Preston. She had thought her initial attraction to Tommy was strong, but what she was feeling now was even stronger. Strong enough to be almost jolting. When she glanced his way, the very air seemed to thicken, and her body hummed with a yearning she hadn't felt in a long time.

But of course, she told herself, that was simply because he was new to her. An unknown. Her fright was probably feeding into it. Adrenaline, she knew, could do odd things to a person.

There was really no point in avoiding it. No one would ever know about the heaviness that settled between her legs when she thought about Creed. It was a secret she could easily keep, and she might as well enjoy it because she had begun to think Tommy had killed that part of her forever.

A short time later, the throbbing heaviness seemed to fill her, and it turned to a drowsiness that captured her and carried her away into a weird dream of Creed Preston. In her dream, every time she stepped toward him he seemed to melt away into shadow.

* * *

Creed sat facing his computer, tapping impossibly slowly at the keys in close approximation of a human's typing rate, until he heard both Yvonne's heart and breathing slip into the rhythm of sleep. She, of course, would have no idea that she couldn't pretend to sleep around him, that he could smell the sleep hormones, and even the scent of her earlier desire, quieted now in sleep. Her heartbeat reached him more clearly than his own. He could read her moods and sometimes thoughts from her heart rate and her scents. In an emotional sense, she was nearly an open book, even though he couldn't read her mind.

When he was sure she had found deep and restful sleep, he deleted the nonsense he'd been typing and shut down his computer. He couldn't work with her maddening scent in the room. No way. And it was even harder now that he had smelled her sexual response to him.

Locked in an eternal internal struggle between his killer instincts and his determination not to give in to them, he scarcely had room left for complex thought at the moment.

No, he would have liked to launch himself

across the room, bite Yvonne before she even awoke, and take her to that heaven known only to vampires and their victims, the place where near-death and sex combined to make a mortal and an immortal one in a way that could never be explained, only experienced.

And once he did, she would always want more.

That was a burden he wouldn't wish on anyone. Sometimes he saw them, mortals who belonged to vampire cults, who might think that every "vampire" who drank from them was merely playing a game, but who had been drunk from by a real vampire, drunk from sufficiently that the craving to repeat the experience gripped them as surely as cocaine addiction. And as devastatingly.

It was possible to drink only a small amount, to briefly sate the insatiable craving for warm living blood, and leave a mortal pleased but intact, without a perpetual craving for more. But some vampires didn't bother, and Creed had seen the results in haunted faces in the nightclubs that catered to their fetish, giving themselves too freely and too quickly to strangers in hopes they would again find that rush.

He wouldn't do that to anyone.

And he certainly wouldn't do it to a woman who had turned to him for protection. Nor would he appreciate being wanted in that way. After all, he remembered the real love of a real woman, the joys of having a family. Pure lust and addiction would never measure up.

But the craving was so deeply rooted in his nature he could be free of it only in death.

So he sat staring out over the sleeping city and the incredible colors the night held for him, listening to a woman's heartbeat, and wondering how he had been chosen for this fate.

Because he didn't believe in accidents. He hadn't been chosen at random by some hungry vampire. No, he'd been chosen by a woman who knew him, knew he had a family, and had taken him away from them anyway to fulfill her own desires.

No accident that. She could have chosen anyone, but she had wanted *him*. The irony, of course, was that she had never really gotten him. What she had gotten was a furious newborn vampire who had wanted to kill her when he found out what he had become. A vampire who had never forgiven her for depriving him of every single thing he cared about.

That memory, that fury, had eventually schooled him to contain his needs, desires and drives. And he'd be damned if he would do that to Yvonne, no matter how much he craved her.

But God, he craved her more than he'd ever craved anything since his change.

If this was a test, he teetered on the edge of failing it miserably.

Finally, in desperation, he went into his bedroom and locked himself safely within. In here her smell would dissipate. In here he could no longer hear her heartbeat.

Rarely did he retire before dawn, but this night he could do nothing else. He picked up a novel he had started reading a few weeks ago, and settled in a chair to wait for the prickling on the back of his neck that would warn him of the approach of the sleep of death.

Until then, he could not afford to think about the delicious morsel lying on his couch.

Trusting him.

He had to remember that: she trusted him.

He could not, would not, betray her.

Chapter 3

Yvonne leaned back from her laptop as dusk began to settle over the city, and she realized she was growing increasingly edgy. Edgy at being alone all day in a virtual stranger's apartment. Edgy that the night might bring some answers to her when Jude arrived. Edgy that she couldn't just go home and be safe.

Indeed, whatever *it* was, it had deprived her of that most basic human need: a home.

And Creed, much as he attracted her, was an odd bird indeed. Not just his illness—a quick online search had even given her the name for it—but odd in that while he had food in his fridge, a fridge too clean to be believed, and food in his cupboards, none of it was opened or used. Despite his invitation, she had hesitated to open those packages until hunger drove her to it.

Of course, she might be making too much of it. He might have just had it all delivered, but it *did* seem odd that not one thing was open except the coffee, and he'd opened that bag last night.

She didn't know anybody who finished everything in the cupboard before restocking. There was always an open box of cereal, or crackers or something in the cupboard or fridge. Always.

He must be the ultimate clean freak. Or maybe he ate out, and just kept food on hand in case.

She sighed and stretched widely, loosening muscles that had tensed from hours bent over her computer. At least her writing had gone well. Very well.

But with only the sounds of the city to keep her company all day, even though she was not alone, another kind of tension seemed to have crept in. Nothing like the feeling in her condo of course, but tension nonetheless.

A bad feeling loomed over her, and she hated it, especially when all she had to point to was that unnerving sense of not being alone in her condo. Was she losing her mind?

No, she reminded herself. Creed had sensed it, too. And then insisted that pewter plate had been thrown at him. Much as she wanted to dismiss it, she couldn't. That plate was too heavy to move on its own, nor had it been set in such a way that it could just fall. But every time she told herself he must have been kidding, she remembered the look on his face. *He* believed it had been thrown. So either he was totally crazy or it was true. Believing him crazy would have been easy except for what she had already experienced herself, especially last night.

Of course, he was beginning to seem a little less like a paragon of sanity, given the state of his fridge. The darn things never looked that clean and his looked as if it had never really been used.

A quiet little laugh escaped her at her own ridiculous thoughts, just as she heard the door behind her open. She swiveled immediately and saw Creed emerge from his bedroom. It was just now dusk, she hadn't yet turned on any lights, and he appeared like a mysterious figure, almost otherworldly.

"Good evening," he said.

"Hi."

"Did your day go well?" He asked the question as he bent to turn on a lamp. Now that he no longer appeared quite so mysterious, she noted that he apparently awoke looking every bit as awake and put together as he had the night before. No sleep-puffed eyes, no helter-skelter hair.

"Fine," she answered, summoning a smile. "I was just calling it a day on my work."

"I hope you found enough to eat."

Which led her to the question that had bothered her all day. "Don't you ever eat at home? I couldn't find anything open."

He paused. "Well, actually, I mostly keep food on hand for guests. I'm no cook and when I want something I just order it. I hope you didn't hesitate to open things so you could eat."

"Well, not for long. I got too hungry."

"Good."

Suddenly realizing she was being rude, she

hopped up from her chair. “You must want your desk back.”

“Not yet. Relax. Jude will probably be here shortly, and I hate to get involved in something and then have to stop.”

She nodded, understanding that feeling well.

He came farther into the living area—almost cautiously, she thought—and settled on an armchair. Was he afraid of frightening her? If anything about him frightened her, it was her attraction to him. It seemed to be growing, and she wished she knew of some way to bridge the distance between them. Of course, that assumed he found her attractive, too. Maybe he didn’t, despite what he had said last night as they were leaving the elevator. He wouldn’t be the first guy to feel that way.

She sighed.

“Something wrong?”

“Other than that I can’t go home? Not a thing.” And not entirely true.

“If anyone can take care of your problem, it’s Jude,” he said firmly.

She wandered closer and sat on the couch, still made up as a bed because she hadn’t been sure whether to fold things up. Folding them up would make more work for Creed if she needed to stay here another night. "You have a lot of confidence in Jude."

"I've seen what he can do. And what it costs him. I have every confidence in him."

"What does it cost him?"

"What does it cost a homicide detective? Or in Terri's case, a medical examiner? Some jobs just leave scars."

She nodded, not knowing how to respond. "I hope I meet Terri eventually."

"I'm sure you will. She's a very likable lady. You mentioned writing. What kind do you do?"

"I'm a novelist. I write fantasy, usually."

"So you create worlds?"

"One mostly. I write a series."

"Six-legged blue cows?"

She had to laugh. "I try not to jar my readers that way. The trick is making the world seem close enough to the one we live in so that it seems familiar, yet different enough to establish that it *is* another world."

"That would be an interesting challenge. Tolkien did it incredibly well."

"Something to aspire to, certainly. But most

of us don't have the luxury of spending the better part of a lifetime creating one world."

"His command of the language was impressive, especially. A true storyteller's voice. I can pick up any of those books, start reading at any point, and become totally absorbed again. Some day you'll have to tell me one of your titles."

"Not if you're going to compare me to Tolkien."

He smiled, certainly one of the most attractive smiles she'd ever seen. Had her heart skipped a beat? Thank goodness he couldn't possibly know.

"What makes you so certain I'd be critical?"

"Nobody measures up to Tolkien."

"Well, if you take that as a given, you don't need to be concerned, do you?"

"Are you always impeccably logical?"

This time he laughed, a warm, rolling sound. "It's the job. It creeps into the rest of my life."

"I never met anyone who worked for a think tank before."

"Think of it as being a highly paid professor. The job isn't really very different, except I don't teach. I spend my nights reading, researching, pondering ideas, putting bits and pieces together into some kind of coherence and insight. Apparently I succeed well enough that they keep on paying me."

"That's always a good sign."

"I generally take it that way."

Just then his cell phone rang. He pulled it out of his slacks pocket and flipped it open. "Yes, Gray? Send them up, please. Oh, and add them to my always welcome list if you don't mind. Thanks."

He closed the phone. "You'll get your wish to meet Terri. She's coming with Jude."

That relieved Yvonne. Jude had struck her as every bit as intense and somehow unnerving as Creed. She understood why Creed unnerved her; she was attracted to him. She didn't feel at all attracted to Jude, yet he left her subtly uneasy. If Pat Matthews hadn't recommended him, she probably would have looked for someone else to investigate what was going on in her apartment.

Although she frankly couldn't imagine who. Calling some paranormal group to come in and tell her she wasn't imagining it, wave their meters around and claim her condo was haunted, wasn't her idea of a solution. No, she had to believe that whatever was behind this could be dealt with, no matter the means.

Creed answered the door, admitting Jude and a beautiful young woman with inky black hair and bright blue eyes. A tiny woman, not at all what Yvonne had expected in a medical examiner. Somehow she had thought they must all be big, strong and powerful. So much for stereotyping.

Terri greeted her warmly with a beautiful smile and handshake. Jude was more restrained, and it didn't escape her notice that he and Creed sat at the far end of the living room, while Terri joined her on the couch, still made up as a bed.

Or that Terri immediately took her hand. "Yvonne, I want you to know something."

"Yes?"

"I've had experiences like the ones you're having. One of them went on for years when I was a kid."

"How did you stand it?"

"For a long time I convinced myself I was imagining it. Eventually too much happened to believe that anymore. Things started being moved. It called my name. And one night it ripped the blankets off me."

Yvonne gasped in horror. "My God! I don't think I could handle that."

"It wasn't a matter of handling it. I was scared to death. I freaked."

"I would, too. I'm freaked already just by the feeling that something is watching me."

Terri squeezed her hand as Jude spoke. "We need to deal with it. And we will. But I need your permission to go into your apartment, Yvonne, and bring Garner with me."

"To set up equipment?"

Jude shook his head. "We have other means. If there's such a thing as a bloodhound for evil, Garner's it. He has a gift for sensing these things, and if there's any way to follow it, he'll be able to do it."

Yvonne's heart started hammering uncomfortably. Why did Creed's nostrils seem to flare suddenly? There was something weird about these guys. But even as she had the thought, she decided that weird or not, they couldn't approach the craziness she'd been experiencing for the last week. "What do you think this thing is?"

"A demon," Jude said.

Yvonne sat stunned. Admittedly over the past week she'd reached the point of considering a not-very-pleasant ghost, but a *demon?* Her heart skipped several beats, then slammed hard enough to feel. "Demon? I don't believe in demons! That's…that's…"

"I told you," Creed said quietly. "There are some things you can't believe in until you meet them."

Yvonne desperately sought Terri with her eyes and saw both understanding and acceptance there. "Have you met one?"

Terri nodded. "It…almost killed Jude."

At that point, Yvonne became utterly convinced that someone was lying to her about something. Terri's hesitation, as if choosing her words carefully. Creed and Jude sitting across the room like a pair of inscrutable twins who didn't want to get close to her. Not even within arm's reach. As if they were afraid of her? How could anyone fear her?

She jumped up from the couch and stood where she could face them all, her arms folded as much for self-protection as anything. The edginess she'd been feeling all day seemed to be coalescing, especially around these three. As if they were unwilling to share information. As if… Oh, hell, something about those two men didn't feel right. Something was *off* and she couldn't ignore it any longer.

"How am I supposed to trust you if you keep secrets from me?" she asked. "There's something you're not telling me. And you're acting as if…as if I stink! As if *you're* afraid of *me*."

Terri answered her. "What makes you think we're hiding something?"

"I keep getting this feeling that there's subtext going on and you're excluding me. Especially," she added, pointing at Creed, "from *you*. Your refrigerator looks as if no one lives here. No open food boxes in your cupboard. First you shy from me and then tell me I'm wrong about your reaction. But every time I get near you, you stiffen or back away."

She gasped, because all of a sudden, so fast she couldn't believe it had happened, Creed was standing in front of her. "How did you do that?" she whispered.

"It's easy," he said tautly. "I'm not afraid of *you*. I'm afraid of myself."

Her jaw dropped open. "How… What…?"

Terri came close. "The key to your apartment? Jude and I will leave you to discuss this."

Creed answered without ever taking his eyes from Yvonne. "She left it on the étagère by the bedroom door."

How had he remembered that? She hadn't even remembered that. And why were his eyes no longer golden? Why did they look as dark as the depths of hell?

And why couldn't she look away from him? It was as if the entire universe had narrowed to his eyes. She barely heard the other two leave.

"Yvonne. I'm going to tell you something. I'm going to tell you because I loathe lying, so once, just once, I'm going to tell you the truth. You're not going to believe me. And then when you don't, I'm going to try to make you forget I told you."

"Why?" Her heart had begun to pound wildly, and she saw his nose flare, his eyes grow even darker. Confusion and inexplicable fright flooded her, yet also mesmerized her. Some force called to her even as instincts tried to tell her to flee.

"Because it's dangerous to me for you to

know. But if I tell you, even if you forget, at some level you'll know I've withheld nothing."

She wished she could tear her gaze from his, but it seemed impossible. "This doesn't make sense."

"It doesn't have to make sense. It just is. So listen to me very carefully. You won't believe me, but I'm telling you the truth. I am a vampire."

"Oh, sure…" But her voice trailed away. The way he looked at her, the change in his eyes. She had the sense that even as they were trying to help her, they were withholding an important piece of the puzzle. The clean fridge. The way he tried to stay away from her. And, just now, the way he had managed to cross the room, one instant in his chair, the very next standing in front of her. Like a magician's trick.

But mostly it was those dark-as-night eyes. Panic replaced fright. Because she believed him. No proof, nothing except those eyes.

And she believed him. "Oh, my God." It was a thin whisper.

"So now you know," he said. Then his voice took on a different timbre. "Forget what I just told you. You don't need to remember it. I'm no threat to you. So forget."

She stood there staring at him, her heart racing like a trip hammer. "I won't forget," she said finally, little more than a cracked whisper.

And then as if someone had cut her strings, she collapsed on the couch and sat staring at the floor.

He was a vampire. And she believed it.

Now how the hell was she supposed to deal with that?

Chapter 4

Creed stared at her in utter perplexity. Not all humans, of course, were amenable to being vamped. Not every human could be controlled by the Voice. But this one… She believed him. He had been so certain that she would get mad, believe he was telling another lie, or just forget he'd even said it.

Now what the hell was he going to do? And how was it possible she believed so readily what almost no one else in the modern world believed anymore?

He racked his brains, wondering what he had done that had convinced her. Her comments about the food really amounted to nothing. His avoidance of her had been countered by his truthful insistence that he didn't find her repulsive at all.

He happened to glance toward a glass-fronted bookcase and then he knew: his eyes had gone as black as night.

Sighing, he retreated to the far end of the living room and wondered how best to handle this so that whenever Jude cleared her apartment she could go on with her life.

He watched her sitting there all curled in on herself and wondered why people always wanted the truth when the truth so often appalled them. Why couldn't they just be happy with polite social fictions?

Well, he admitted, most people probably were. But not this one. She'd clearly sensed something, and hadn't been willing to let it go.

Which left them here and now. He cleared his throat. Slowly she lifted her head and looked at him. She still hadn't recovered from the shock, and he missed the usual spark in her green eyes.

"I hope," he said, "that you won't share my secret."

"Who would believe me?"

Good question. He chose not to answer directly. "*You* believed me."

"After what's been going on in my condo for a week, I'm ready to believe in almost anything. Why the hell wouldn't I believe in a vampire?"

"Because almost nobody believes in us anymore."

She gave a short laugh, absolutely humorless. "Your secret is safe with me. I wouldn't want to get myself committed. Or wind up on your menu."

"I told you I won't hurt you."

"No? Don't vampires survive by killing?"

"Not me. Not Jude."

Her head jerked sharply at that. "Why should you be any different?"

"I guess I still have some human hang-ups."

Her eyes widened, and he saw with relief that a hint of the spark had returned.

He let her have some silence, some space to think whatever she needed to think about this. Finally she looked at him again. "Jude, too?"

He nodded.

"Terri?"

He shook his head.

"But she's his wife. How can she not be?"

"He won't change her. Says he wants to be absolutely certain she knows what she's getting into."

Her brow knit. "Are you telling me it's awful?"

"That depends on what you focus on, and what you're willing to give up. I didn't choose this. It was forced on me and cost me every damn thing I cared about. So whether you want to believe it or not, I would never do this to anyone else."

"Never is a long time."

"I have a lot of never ahead of me."

She looked down again, and he let her be. The questions would come when the questions came, and at some point she was going to decide he must have lied. And that thought pained him. Odd that after a century he still needed acceptance for who and what he was, just as he was. He ought to be used to the mess he called his life by now.

"So," she said finally, looking at him. "Why did you tell me, especially when it could be dangerous to you?"

"Because I get sick of the lies. I hate lying."

"And you were sure you could make me forget." Her tone was accusatory.

"Not sure. It doesn't always work." He waited, the night minutes ticking by, minutes he hated to waste because he couldn't extend them by much. But she needed the time to adjust, and he was smart enough to know it.

Little by little she seemed to be relaxing. Adapting. Accepting. He had no idea where that would lead, but it was a vast improvement over the edginess he'd felt in her since he'd awakened this evening.

For the first time since shock had caused her to sag onto the couch, she did more than glance at him. Her gaze met his directly, steadily. Her tone took on an edge of tartness. "This is so very cool. In one day I learn there are demons and vampires both. I am just *thrilled*."

Her tone prevented him from taking offense. Indeed, he wouldn't have blamed her if she'd turned hysterical or accused him of being lying scum. By comparison, this was a mild reaction. "I know it's hard."

"Hard?" A short laugh escaped her. "Somehow I think it ought to be harder. But after the past week, I'd probably believe in werewolves, too."

"Um..." He drew the sound out and hesitated. Her eyes grew big again.

"No," she said.

"Afraid so."

"Oh, my God." She closed her eyes, but only a second or two passed before they snapped open again, intent now. "How much of the myth is true? Are you immortal?"

"Near enough. I die every morning and resurrect every night."

"Why do you keep backing away from me?"

"Because you smell so good to me. Regardless of how I choose to live, Yvonne, I'm still a predator. Nothing will ever change that."

"You want to kill me?" She looked appalled.

"I want to drink from you. There's a difference. I wouldn't kill you. That's not necessary, and certainly not desirable. But yes, I want you in ways you can't imagine."

She caught her breath, and stared at him wide-eyed. "Do you feel that way about every human?"

"Not quite. There are some who are more

enticing than others. You're the most enticing morsel I've ever met."

"Oh." She twisted her fingers together. "As a meal?"

"In *every* way."

Her eyes widened, and then that maddening blush came to her cheeks. It called to him, to his hunger and his lust, as little had. He closed his eyes, seeking self-control even as his body hummed with need. She would never begin to imagine how hard it was, nor did he ever want her to.

But apart from his instincts, he was quite sure he wanted her to move on before he came to care about her as any more than as a passing acquaintance or a tempting delicacy. He'd lost everything he'd ever loved, and he wasn't going there again. Ever.

But even as the tension seemed to leave her, as she appeared to accept this new blow, he watched her drop her head in her hands. More minutes passed, then she said almost plaintively, "Why in the world would I have a demon in my condo?"

"I don't know." He rubbed his chin, as if the mere rubbing of it could erase the delicious aroma of that woman, or keep it from reaching his extremely sensitive nose. “You haven’t done anything have you? Held a séance, used a Ouija board?”

“No, I wouldn’t dabble with that stuff.” She appeared faintly embarrassed. “I don’t know how much I believe in it, but I don’t see any reason to run that kind of risk.”

“I agree with you there.”

She paused, suddenly looking thoughtful. “I’ve never done anything like that. But my ex-boyfriend might have.”

His attention perked and he moved a bit closer. “Why do you say that?”

“I’m not even sure if he did. He had all these necklaces he’d wear from time to time, even though I hated some of them. Everything from an Iron Cross to some kind of feathers he said were an old talisman, to a star, and I didn’t think much of it. Well, that’s not exactly true. I objected to the Iron Cross, and the feathers kind of stank. But what’s to object to in a star?”

Then she gasped, apparently making a connection, and spoke quickly. “It wasn’t just a star. It was a pentagram. Why the hell didn’t I realize that?" Her eyes narrowed, even as her hands clenched into fists.

"Oh, man." She barely breathed the words. Then she spoke acidly. "Oh, wouldn't that be just like Tommy and his friends. To think something like that was cool. They'd love the idea it would upset some people. Heck, they'd probably even think it made them special and different."

"When did you break up with him?"

"About two months ago. I found out he was cheating on me." Her voice broke and then steadied. Clearly it still hurt like hell to remember the discovery. "And frankly, I didn't like some of his friends. The cheating was the last straw." She shook her head. "Anyway, his friends were…well…it's hard to explain. I'm pretty sure they were doing some drugs, which I didn't like, but their behavior grated on me. Cynical, antisocial and determined to break rules for the sake of breaking them. Arrested development." She sighed. "And they seemed to be rubbing off on Tommy. He wasn't like that at first, Creed. Truly he wasn't. But after we'd been together about four or five months, he started bringing them home with him from the club where he had a gig."

"I believe you," he said gently.

"He changed." Her voice broke again. "I blamed his friends, but maybe I didn't really know him. Could somebody really change that much just because of friends? But he seemed to be getting more like them as time passed."

"Did he start wearing that star necklace more often?"

She frowned faintly. "I don't know. He started wearing his necklaces under his shirt so I wouldn't see them. It made me mad that he still wore them when he knew I didn't like some of them, but it made me mad at myself, too, for objecting to the stupid things. I mean, I must have seemed like such a bitch, picking on his jewelry."

Creed sat, rubbing his chin slowly, lost in thought. There could definitely be a link, he thought, but how much of one he couldn't be sure. The gateway, if they'd opened one, would have been where she lived before, not where she lived now. He definitely needed to kick this around with Jude, but for the moment he didn't want to add to Yvonne's worries, so he asked no more questions.

Yvonne, however, broke into his thoughts with a question of her own.

"You said your relative was attacked?"

"My great-granddaughter. She was nearly killed."

She hesitated, then said, "That's mind-blowing."

"What is?"

"You don't look anywhere near old enough to have a great-granddaughter."

"I told you I was married once, and had daughters."

"I know, but… Sorry, none of my business."

"I was married, I had four daughters and a son. And then some damn vampire decided she wanted me, changed me and I was never able to go back to them."

The corners of her mouth drew down. "They couldn't accept you?"

"I wouldn't ask them to. And certainly not in the state I was in at first. So I watched from afar, watched them grow old and die."

"I'm so sorry! I can't imagine the pain."

He closed his eyes again, this time to blind

himself to her sympathy. He hadn't expected that. "It was a long time ago," he said finally. "A very long time ago."

"Feelings," she said quietly, "have their own calendar. They don't vanish simply because the months and years turn over."

His eyes snapped open. "No. They don't. But they visit less often, though they remain every bit as strong."

She nodded. "I know. I lost my mother five years ago. Not that long in terms of pain, even when you don't especially like them. I can only imagine what it must have been like to stay away when they were still there."

He felt utterly flabbergasted. First she accepted that he was a vampire as if he hadn't just bent all the rules of her known reality, and now she was expressing sympathy rather than fear or revulsion. "You are quite…unusual."

"Why? Because I'm not running in screaming terror?"

"Because you believe what I told you and now you're expressing sympathy."

"Your eyes," she said simply. "The way they changed. How could I not believe? I felt something already. Something different. You moved so fast and then your eyes changed. There's no other explanation than that you're telling me the truth."

"I am. But I still would have expected some difficulty."

"You mean I should get upset, scream, deny, whatever?" She shrugged. "Maybe most people would. I'm weird. I've always been weird. And I like unusual people. You certainly qualify as the most unusual person I've ever met."

One corner of his mouth drew up. "So you think of me as a person? I'm not even a human anymore."

"You're still a person." She leaned back and tucked her legs up beneath her on the couch. "I write about all kinds of fantastic beings. Some come from tradition, myth and fairy tales, others I make up. But I've never followed the current trend for vampires and werewolves." She half smiled. "You're giving me ideas for a story."

"About vampires?"

"Maybe. You're not at all what I would have expected."

"Meaning?"

"Vampire as St. George."

Finally he laughed and allowed himself to relax. Things might change at any instant as she truly absorbed what he'd told her, but for the moment he was willing to enjoy himself. At least as much as he could when her scent was driving him nuts. "I'm no saint, and certainly not a dragon-slayer."

"Just don't tell me there are dragons."

"I haven't met one, so I can't say for sure."

A smile flickered across her face. "True. Having just made the acquaintance of a couple of vampires I guess there's no way to be sure that there aren't any dragons, or elves, or trolls."

She was definitely taking this entirely too well. A new and different tension began to creep through him, apart from the tension of self-control. None of her reactions seemed quite normal. The resistance had passed too quickly. The acceptance bordered on the extreme. Most people fought so hard to keep their beliefs about reality intact that they could literally erase from their minds anything that didn't fit. He knew that effect intimately, as he'd seen it in action more than once, and more often than not took advantage of it. Denial was a basic trait of human nature. It actually helped vampires to survive.

Vampires and other things he would not mention, not today. Yvonne was dealing with enough. Or not dealing as the case might be. He honestly wondered which it was.

Her face had grown thoughtful, and he tensed again, waiting to hear her thoughts. He couldn't help feeling that her easy acceptance of what he had told her was nothing but a ticking time bomb that might go off at any moment.

But then she looked up at him with a crooked smile. "I could use a little more proof, I think."

"Proof that I'm a vampire?"

"Yes. Part of me recognizes that you moved far too fast for a human, that your eyes change in a way I've never seen any human's do. But another part of me is seriously balking."

"I'm honestly surprised that you aren't terrified, given the stories everyone tells about us."

She gave a little shake of her head. "You've been kind to me in the extreme. I tend to judge people by their actions even more than their words. I'm not afraid of *you*."

"Maybe you should be."

Her eyes widened a bit, and for the first time he saw a hint of fear that had nothing to do with what was going on in her apartment. Yes, it was better if she kept a distance, but his chest tightened anyway.

"Are you threatening me or warning me?" she asked.

In an instant he hovered over her, bending so close that he could feel the warmth of her breath, itself an intoxicant. "I'm a predator," he whispered in her ear. "I can control myself. But with you… You have no idea how much I'd like to taste you."

He heard her suck a sharp breath, then release it in a long sigh. He knew the reaction she was having. Many had it in the presence of a vampire. Burgeoning sexual interest, an almost soporific relaxation. Next she'd turn her head to expose her neck and he'd hate himself just for revealing that she was as helpless before the attraction of his kind as any other human. He didn't want to see her that way, but he also didn't want to examine his reasons for that.

She surprised him, though. She didn't offer her neck. She didn't adopt a pose of compliance. No, she raised her hand and touched his cheek, electrifying him with her warmth, the only warmth he could feel anymore.

"It must be hard for you," she said. "I should go to a hotel."

Appalled, he straightened instantly, crossing the room so fast that she couldn't have seen him move. "No," he said. "No. I don't want you to be alone."

"But this is causing you problems. And you can't do anything about it anyway. Can you? Jude can do just as much if I'm in a hotel."

"No," he said again, feeling his body coil as if it wanted to spring. Only with huge effort did he avoid crouching a bit. "It won't be safe for you. I can handle it. And yes, my very presence helps protect you."

"How?"

"Because if anything tries to take you, it'll have to deal with me. They don't like to deal with my kind, Yvonne. We're beyond their reach and we can wreak havoc on them when they take physical form. And…I could drag you back from the gateway of hell."

His doorbell rang, interrupting further discussion much to his relief. He'd said more than he intended, and things he didn't want to explain.

He went to let Jude and Terri back in. He noted the way they both looked at Yvonne, but only Terri's face betrayed surprise.

"You're not upset?" she said to Yvonne.

"About the existence of vampires? Why would I be? There are worse predators in the world evidently."

Jude looked at Creed. "She doesn't get it."

"I'm not sure about that."

"I don't get what?" Yvonne demanded.

Jude looked at her. "That we *could* be the worst predators on the planet. If we chose to."

"Do some of you?"

Creed felt a dark wave of bitterness. "Some do. Like the one who changed me. As a rule, most of us prefer not to make a bloody mess of things because like you, we prefer feeling reasonably safe."

"Well, then." That seemed to settle it for Yvonne. "At the moment I'm more troubled by what's going on in my condo."

"That," said Terri, "is something I agree with. Totally."

"She does have a point," Jude agreed. "That

feeling isn't plaguing her because some prurient boyfriend or neighbor has installed miniature cameras or listening devices. Whatever it is, it's big and it's bad. I just wish I knew why it's interested in Yvonne."

Creed spoke. "Yvonne may have just shed some light on that. I'm not certain, nor is she, but her former boyfriend may have had some connection to Satanism."

Yvonne spoke quickly, surprising Creed with her defense of Tommy after the bitter way she'd spoken of him. But old loyalties died hard, as he knew well. "And he might have just worn that upside-down star the same way he wore the Iron Cross—to bother people."

Creed acknowledged her point with a nod. "Perhaps."

"Was it a real Iron Cross?" Jude asked. "Or just a Greek Cross."

"He said it was a real one, that he got it in some antique store. It came in a box with a ribbon and he put it on a necklace."

"Hmm." Now Jude looked thoughtful.

"Does it make a difference?" Yvonne asked.

"Only as it pertains to his psychology," Creed answered. "It's a decoration, like any other military decoration. In and of itself, nothing but a mark of courage or some memorable deed. But wearing it, given its connotations because of the Holocaust and the war, says something."

"That's what bothered me," Yvonne said slowly. "I suppose people aren't as sensitive to that today, though."

"Sensitive enough that your boyfriend wore it."

"Meaning?"

"What could he have wanted it for otherwise? An old military decoration."

He watched her fall into thought again and realized that he liked the way she did that. He wasn't accustomed to being around people anymore, but even less so around people who weren't afraid to just stop talking and think about things.

"There could be other reasons," she said slowly.

"Could be." He wasn't going to argue with her about it. Absolutely nothing could be gained.

But then she looked up and gave him an almost rueful smile. "Why am I defending him?

I left him because I found some of his behavior truly troubling and because he cheated on me. But here I am trying to defend him. That's crazy."

"That's natural," Terri said. "We have a hard time coming to terms with the fact that we cared for someone who probably wasn't worthy of our feelings. Or our respect."

Yvonne's answer was wry. "I think you just hit the nail on the head."

But Creed's thoughts had begun to wander down another path. "How angry was he that you left? Did he make any threats?"

"Just bluster. He said I'd regret it. He said he had ways to get even that I couldn't begin to imagine. But he never actually threatened me physically."

"It's not physical threats I'm worried about." Creed looked at Jude, who nodded.

"I agree," Jude said. Then he flipped open his phone and punched a button. "Garner. Get your butt over here to Creed's place. I need you to do some sniffing around. Yes, now." He closed the phone and shook his head. "Why would that boy think I meant anything else?

He knows as well as anyone that time is of the essence."

Yvonne spoke. "Do you have a lot of trouble with Garner?"

"Actually," Jude answered, "I have less trouble *with* Garner than *because* of him. Sometimes I think he brings the ten plagues along with him."

Then Jude pinned her with his gaze. "So you have no trouble accepting that we're vampires?"

"Not yet."

"Hmm."

"What hmm?"

Creed watched with interest.

"Well," Jude said, "Terri here went after me with my own sword."

Terri giggled, but then added, "Well, actually, I think I may have been… Oh, it was weird, Yvonne. First I believed it, then I didn't believe it. I'm a scientist, and I had a lot of trouble with the notion after the first reaction."

"A sword? Really?" Yvonne's eyes had widened, but then she giggled, too. "I wish I could have seen it."

"I'm sure I looked ridiculous," Terri answered. "But then the doubts set in." She sat next to Yvonne again. "They probably will for you, too."

"At the moment," Yvonne replied, "given whatever is in my apartment, I'm finding it easy to believe a whole lot. What *is* in my apartment?"

Jude answered. "It's not there now."

"But what is it and why do you want Garner?" Her tone had grown impatient, and Creed could well understand. She kept asking what *it* was, and nobody gave her an answer.

"I want Garner because he can pick up the trail at your apartment and follow it. As to what it is..." Jude hesitated then looked at Creed. "You remember what we've been talking about for the past couple of months?"

"That something very powerful was trying to create a gateway? That it needed five possessions to create it?"

Jude nodded, then returned his attention to Yvonne. "There are some powers than can only get through to this world by creating a metaphysical pentagram."

"What's that?"

"It uses lesser demons to possess five people,

then brings these people together to form five localized points on a pentagram. The power generated by those people creates a gateway, usually through the offering of a blood sacrifice."

Yvonne swallowed visibly. "What…" She cleared her throat. "What kind of power are you talking about?"

"The kind that has names you might recognize. In this case I think it might be Asmodai."

The name clearly meant nothing to her. "But why in the world would it be in my condo? I don't fool around with that stuff."

"You may not fool with it," Creed said. "But someone has fooled with something, all right." He rose and went to the étagère to get a manila envelope. Yvonne vaguely remembered him carrying it out of her apartment last night, but had been too upset and frightened to even think about it.

"You need to look at these," Creed said, handing the envelope to Jude. "I found these hidden away in Yvonne's condo."

At once the condo seemed to chill and she felt the watcher again. It was like an icy whisper at the nape of her neck, but quickly gone.

* * *

As soon as the items spilled from the envelope, Asmodai felt them, was drawn to them. And what it found was not pleasing to it. The woman it wanted was there, but so was the vampire it had tried to drive away last night. And so was another. As it focused its attention on them, it could make out their words. They knew too much, it decided. Too much. But it could not yet act in more than small ways in their world, and maddening as it was to have to bide its time a while yet, it had no choice.

Unless it could find another ally, one who could be swayed more easily. One in emotional turmoil that would make it easy to manipulate. It zoomed its attention outward, seeking some weakened being that could be turned on those two vampires.

In its present state, it knew no limits of distance, and only a few in time. It hunted now, seeking one it could use to its ends. One who could stand against a vampire.

Then it found what it wanted, and it summoned the undead being named Luc, calling him with the promises he wanted: promises of vengeance. Making it even more delicious was the fact it had once already stolen what the being most loved. So he would come seeking vengeance, only to be used by it, the thing he most hated.

Ah, they were so easy to manipulate, these paltry beings. It could use them all as pawns, and they would never know. It had tricked them before, when they thought they had tricked it.

Such as the time Solomon had bound it and forced it to build the Temple. But it had bided its time then, and taken its vengeance on Solomon eventually, even ruling in his stead. Not even Raphael had been able to bind it permanently, although it was still annoyed that it had lost the lovely Sarah as a result.

But that was long ago, and when it looked now at Yvonne, it saw a suitable replacement for Sarah, a human woman who stirred a hunger that had been somnolent for millennia.

Patience, it counseled itself.

Patience was its greatest friend, and patient for now it would be.

With some self-satisfaction, it settled back to watch its plans unfold.

Yvonne watched uneasily, rubbing her arms against an inexplicable chill as Jude emptied the envelope onto Creed's dining table. "I've never seen those before." Odd little twists of sticks and bits of dull cloth, strange shapes.

Creed turned to her. "No, I'm sure you haven't. They were well hidden, and I discovered them only because I could smell them."

Yvonne's eyes widened, then she gaped as Jude picked up each piece and sniffed it.

"Yes," he said. "My guess is Asmodai, and someone put these things there for him as a marker."

Yvonne shuddered and rubbed her arms. "Someone was in there? To put that stuff in my apartment? God!" Then a split second later, she said, "Tommy. My God, it had to have been Tommy. I gave the movers the keys to both places. He could have borrowed one. Who the hell else would have wanted to put those things in my condo? And who the hell is Asmodai?"

Jude sighed and looked at Creed. "I believe you know the story."

Creed nodded, feeling a chilly anger begin to trickle through him. "Asmodai makes more than one appearance in ancient writings. But the most significant is his appearance in the Book of Tobit, where he possesses a young woman named Sarah and causes her to kill each of her husbands on their wedding night. Scholars still debate the matter, but general agreement is that Asmodai falls in love with human women."

"Oh, my God," Yvonne breathed. "Oh, my God."

"Put your head down," Terri said swiftly, pressing on the back of Yvonne's neck until she put her head between her knees.

"Have you felt watched before?" Jude asked.

"Jude," Terri scolded. "Give her a minute."

"No, no…" Yvonne lifted her head a bit, though she didn't straighten, and looked at Jude. "Yes," she said. "A few months ago. Briefly. I brushed it off and it didn't come back until I moved here. And it was nothing like this. Nothing." She lowered her head again.

Creed decided that seeing her as pale as winter moonlight was even harder to endure than seeing her blush. He sprang to his feet, not bothering to conceal his speed, and began pacing. "Can you be sure it's Asmodai?"

"No, of course we can't," Jude answered. "But what I do know is that we're dealing with something well beyond an ordinary demon. It's been leaving its stench around for weeks now. You've smelled it, too, and you recognized it in Yvonne's condo. Right?"

Creed found it almost painful to accept. A demon was one thing. The Prince of Demons was another. The idea that Yvonne might be its target filled him with a kind of rage he hadn't felt since his change. And with the rage came an unwelcome, unfamiliar fear. Something he hadn't felt in a long time, except for when his great-granddaughter had almost died from an attack.

"The point is, it has focused on her. Added to her former boyfriend's threat that he could get even in ways she couldn't imagine..."

Creed nodded reluctantly. "If it could find a way to influence her boyfriend and his friends, it would."

"Exactly," Jude agreed. "Asmodai would be the most likely one to do that. It's his M.O."

"True. But there's more than one reason he could want her."

Jude snorted. "Virgin sacrifices aren't difficult to find, even in today's world. I'm not considering that a primary factor in this fixation."

Yvonne's head snapped up. "Who said I'm a virgin?"

Creed didn't know how to respond to that. Jude evidently decided to leave it alone. Finally Terri spoke. "I gather from what Jude said that a virgin sacrifice is needed to bring this demon through. So, either you or some other young woman is headed for trouble. But Jude is also saying that since virgins aren't difficult to find, it's more likely Asmodai has a different interest in you, one that is of more importance or he wouldn't be watching you all the time."

"Oh." Yvonne didn't look at all comforted.

"Thank you for the translation," Jude drawled. "I never, ever, speculate on the state of a lady's, ah, experience."

Terri laughed. "I love it when you slip back into your lord-of-the-manor airs."

"Never a lord," he reminded them.

"But to the manor born nonetheless," Creed said. Finally he could restrain himself no longer. Grabbing the shreds of his self-control, he went to squat beside Yvonne. After a moment's hesitation, he touched her knee lightly. "It would have to get through me, Yvonne. I won't let it."

She lifted her head and looked at him. "But how can you stop it?"

"Well, demons have a bit of trouble with vampires. And in Jude you've hired the best demon slayer around."

"You can *slay* them?"

"No," Jude answered, "but I can send them back to the pit of hell where they belong. Where the devil is Garner?"

Almost in answer to his question, Creed's cell rang. He pulled it out and answered. "Yes, send him up, Gray. And you may as well add him to my list, as well." He closed the phone, shrugging. "I can always remove Garner later."

Jude snorted. "I doubt he'll give *you* much trouble. He seems to avoid vampires other than me."

"Curious, that," Creed agreed. He squeezed Yvonne's knee gently and then straightened.

Jude spoke. "You stay here with Yvonne while Terri and I go meet Garner and put him on the trail." Then he scooped up all the things that had been in the envelope, tucking them back into its depths and stuffing the envelope into his pocket.

Terri turned to Creed, understanding in her

blue eyes. She touched his arm. "Will you be all right?"

He knew exactly what she meant: could he maintain his control alone with Yvonne? He covered her hand with his briefly, enjoying her human warmth, the only warmth he could feel anymore. "Yes."

She smiled gently and nodded, then followed Jude to the door.

Yes, he could handle it, although all the fear that Yvonne felt had perfumed the room like roses, adding to her enticing natural scent. It called to him, awakening an overpowering sexual tension, an overpowering thirst.

But of course he was alone in that.

Always alone.

"I'll be in my room for a few minutes."

At Creed's words, Yvonne jerked upright. The fear that had been running icy fingers up and down her spine since Creed and Jude explained what they believed was happening, intensified. She didn't want to be alone. "Why?"

Creed, once again a distance away, regarded her from eyes that had darkened. "I need to feed," he said bluntly. "It helps me maintain my control. I doubt you want to see it."

"Please. I don't care. I'm more frightened of being alone right now." She knew she was acting like a baby, but she couldn't help it. The feeling of being watched had just been turned into the kind of threat she had only read about, a kind of threat she would have been happier believing didn't exist. She had to handle that somehow, and being alone at this moment didn't seem like a good way to go. Things that had haunted her in her apartment could find her here just as well. "What if it comes here?" *That momentary feeling from a few short minutes ago seemed to return then whisper away.*

He hesitated. Clearly he wanted to tell her it wouldn't and just as clearly he could not make the promise. Her fear ratcheted up a notch. She wasn't even prepared to consider what it meant that she felt safe with a vampire and not safe alone.

"All right. I just need to get a bag out of my room."

She almost jumped up to follow him, but forced herself to remain on the sofa. Her hands clenched until her nails bit into her palms, yet she hardly felt it.

Thirty seconds later Creed reappeared with a bag in hand. She recognized it immediately. It was exactly the kind of bag they used when she made blood donations. He carried it into the kitchen, slit one corner with a knife and emptied it into a large glass.

Then, carrying the ruby liquid, he returned to the living room and the chair farthest from her. He raised the glass as if in toast, an odd twist to his mouth, and watched her as he took the first swallows.

Should she have been repelled? He seemed to expect it, but she felt nothing at all. Nothing except gratitude that he was so willing to do what he could to ease her fear.

Blood glistened on his lips, and he didn't attempt to hide it. Maybe he was giving her the full treatment in an attempt to see if she would be shocked or horrified. She wasn't. He was just eating. For him blood was food.

When he had drained half the glass, he seemed to believe that she wasn't going to go ballistic on him. He sighed, rose, went to the kitchen where he got a paper napkin out of a drawer. After that, he dabbed his lips each time he sipped.

"How does it taste to you?" she asked, desperate to think about anything except demons.

"Awful, frankly. It's full of anticoagulants, and it's not quite...alive."

Another word chosen to shock her, she was sure. "You must hate it."

"I don't love it, but while the alternative is so much more enjoyable, it sets me free from doing things I wouldn't be proud of."

A shiver ran through her.

"Do you need me to turn the heat up?" he asked instantly.

"No. No. I think, um, I don't know what I think."

"Too many shocks for one evening."

She tried to smile. "And it's still early."

"Don't remind me. I'm not sure either of us can handle any more shocks tonight."

"So that Asmodai thing shocks you, too?"

"It appalls me. Horrifies me. I'd love to believe Jude is wrong. Unfortunately, he seldom is about these things."

"Just who is he, really?"

"Asmodai? Also known as Asmodeus,

Prince of Demons, sometimes confused with Satan who may have never really existed according to scholars." He paused. "Sorry, the professor in me comes out without warning. To put it in the modern vernacular, he's one bad dude."

She managed a small laugh. "I think *bad dude* is a compliment in some circles."

"I don't keep up well enough. As the story goes, it took the Archangel Raphael to bind him."

A shiver ran through her, cold and icky. "Then how is Jude supposed to do it?"

"Jude's an experienced exorcist. I'm inclined to trust him."

"That he'll get rid of this thing?"

"Well, at least send it away. Of course, there's never a guarantee."

Of course there was no guarantee. She wouldn't have believed him if had said there was. "Thank you," she said finally.

"For what?"

"Protecting me." Yvonne looked down, taking a moment to try to absorb more of the earthquake of events that had basically shredded reality. "I feel like I'm in a novel. Someone else's."

"I'm not surprised. It's hard to accept all this."

"How old are you? Really?"

"I've been a vampire for over a hundred years. And I was thirty-four when I was changed."

She didn't even try to imagine it; she knew there was no way she could.

She curled up again on the end of the couch, legs tucked beneath her, and closed her eyes, trying once again to absorb everything, to find a way to settle it down inside herself. But this evening she had experienced not one but two things that would leave her forever changed. Her whole world had been rattled because creatures of myth had become real. Nothing would ever look the same again. Nothing.

These things were only supposed to happen in books.

She opened her eyes again and looked at Creed. Despite what she had learned, she still felt attracted to him. Shouldn't that be wrong?

But then she asked herself what was wrong with it. He might not be human, as he said himself, but to her he seemed human in all the ways that counted. And it was just attraction. Almost heady, actually, the kind of heart-racing pull she hadn't felt in a long time. Not since the early days with Tommy, if even then.

She watched as he finished his drink or whatever he called it and went to the kitchen to wash the glass. He had just set it in the drain rack to dry when the bell rang again.

Taking it for granted, apparently, that he no longer had to pretend to be anything he wasn't, he seemed to disappear from the kitchen and reappear at the door. He opened it and Garner burst in followed by Jude and then Terri.

"I am *not* hunting that thing," Garner insisted.

Creed reappeared beside Yvonne. She felt the whisper of the air move and glanced up to see him standing almost protectively over her.

"It's what you do," Jude said firmly.

"Not Asmodai, I don't. We're talking here about the Prince of Demons. The very dangerous, very deadly kind."

"When did you become concerned about danger?" Jude asked.

"Since now. Since it became more than just

another demon. Do you think I want Asmodai to notice me? Cripes, Jude, I'm not demon-resistant like you vampires. I'm just a mortal, easy prey for something like that."

"So you're saying you can't suss him out without being detected?"

Apparently Jude had said the right thing because Garner bridled. "I should be better than that."

"So what's the problem?"

"I can't be sure I'm better than that when it comes to a demon like Asmodai. He's a little more omniscient than most. Isn't he supposed to know the future?"

"I can anoint you, you know."

Garner threw up his hands. "Yeah. What if it rubs off?"

"Are you going to run?"

Garner glared. "You're always telling me to be sensible. Now that I am you're telling me not to be?"

"I'm saying we have a serious demon problem going here, that at least one woman is at risk, maybe two since a sacrifice is needed to bring Asmodai through, and there are five other people who have been or are about to be possessed. You want to let that happen? You want to let him come through?"

Garner seemed to freeze. After a moment, his shoulders sagged. "All right, all right. I'll look for the people who are possessed. I won't promise to track Asmodai though. Not on purpose. If we can keep him from getting five people, he's off the table anyway."

"This time," Jude said grimly.

Garner shook his head. "Just promise me one thing, Jude?"

"What's that?"

"Finish training Creed. I don't think one exorcist is going to be enough. Not by what I sensed in that apartment."

"Fair enough. I figured I'd need help."

Then Garner surprised Yvonne by approaching her. He stood there for a minute, closing his eyes. Then, "I sense he's been around her, but he's not here now. Not even a fingerprint. Whatever he wants with her, he hasn't gotten to the point of taking it yet." He opened his eyes and looked straight at Yvonne. "Don't go back to your place. Absolutely do not. His presence is strong there. Too strong. I just don't understand why he hasn't touched you yet."

Yvonne felt her heart stop. "Touched me?"

"I hope you never find out." Then Garner stomped toward the door. "Creed, don't leave her alone. Not for a minute."

She looked up at Creed. "What did he mean, touch me?"

"I gather if Asmodai had touched you in any way, Garner would have detected it."

"That's right," Jude agreed. "Those things leave fingerprints behind that Garner can always sense. And if he had managed to touch you, you'd have been changed in some way. This is good news."

"How?" Yvonne demanded.

"He evidently can't reach out yet. Not enough to touch you. And we need to keep it that way."

Yvonne noticed that her fingers hurt, and she looked down to realize that she had knotted them together. With effort, she untangled them and stretched them. "So what now?" she asked.

"Dinner," Terri said brightly. "I know of two humans who need to feed, even if you vampires don't. Order in or go to a restaurant?" Jude looked at her and she laughed. "Somehow I thought that would be your reaction. Preferences, Yvonne?"

"I'm not sure I could eat right now."

"It's not whether you want to. I'm a doctor. Take it from me, you've had enough shocks tonight. You *need* to eat. So what'll it be?"

"Whatever you want. I can't decide." She felt a hand on her shoulder and looked up to see Creed staring down at her, his face creased with concern. She wished she dared reach up and take his hand, but natural reticence held her back. He might not like it.

He squeezed her shoulder gently, then stepped away. "I'll go get you some fresh clothes. Be right back."

Yvonne watched him leave, invisible except when he paused to open the door.

All of a sudden she felt lonely indeed. And more scared than she had ever been in her life.

Chapter 5

"Here's the thing," Creed said to Yvonne after dinner when the others had left.

She looked at him. Food filled her stomach like lead. Something inside her seemed to have deadened. Her eyes felt hot, as if she were crying tearlessly. "Yes?"

"If I'm to keep you with me every minute, then we'll have to share my bedroom. I don't mind. You can have the bed. I won't even notice that I'm on the floor since I'll be dead. I can set you up to work in there. But will it bother you to spend a day locked in with me?"

"What difference will it make where I spend

the day if you're dead?" And how weird did that sound?

"I won't be so dead that I can't wake to deal with a serious threat. I just have to do it in a completely darkened room. Well, you can have a lamp on if you like."

"If you're dead, how can you wake?"

"I can for brief periods if necessary. It's not an easy thing, but I *can* do it if I have to."

"Okay." God, even talking felt like too much of a strain.

Suddenly—he did everything suddenly it seemed now—he sat beside her on the sofa. "Do you mind?"

"Mind what?"

"Having me so close?"

She shook her head, hoping he couldn't tell how her heart had leaped. Hoping he couldn't read on her face just how much she *wanted* him close. "But it bothers *you,* evidently."

"I can control myself. It's hard especially with you, but I can do it."

"What is it about me?"

"I don't know." He shrugged. "It just is. You nearly craze me, frankly. I want you. I want to taste you. I want to—" He broke off sharply. "Bad timing."

"What does timing have to do with anything? Right now the timing of *everything* stinks."

He held out his hand. Yvonne looked at it, noting its ineffable paleness. Was that from death or lack of sun?

But curiosity and longing both twinged deep within her, so she reached out and laid her hand in his. And discovered that he was cool, but not cold, and that his skin was amazingly smooth. His fingers closed gently around hers. "I thought you'd be cold," she said.

"I assume room temperature when I sleep. The rest of the time, slightly warmer. I have a heart that beats, blood that pumps. I'm not dead, just undead."

"So that's why you didn't have the heat on? It doesn't matter to you?"

"Not at all. I'm impervious to temperature. In fact, the only warmth I feel anymore is human warmth. Like the touch of your hand right now."

She looked down at their twined hands and tried to wrap her mind around it. Nothing seemed to click, so she asked tentatively, "Do you miss *being* warm?"

"I don't notice it at all, except at moments like this." He gave her hand a gentle squeeze. "Now I notice. Very much."

"So you drink preserved blood, which you detest, and avoid warmth, which you say you crave. Sorry, Creed, but that sounds terrible."

"It can be."

She felt he was downplaying it, suspected that his change, brought about in such a horrible way, cost him more than his family. A century without warmth and love? Without the food you most wanted? "It sounds like a sentence to hell."

"Ah, damn." He sighed.

"What?"

"It's not. There are times when I could feel miserably sorry for myself if I wanted to. But if ever I can't take it anymore, there's a way out."

"What's that?"

"All I have to do is ask another vampire for mercy."

Maybe she was getting used to the shocks, because only one little ripple of horror passed through her. As a writer, all the nuances of that word struck her. To ask for mercy was to ask for a reprieve from the intolerable. So these vampires didn't simply ask to be killed. They asked for something so much more meaningful. "Mercy? Is that what you call it?"

"It's the word we use when we can't take it anymore. The request is always granted."

"So you kill each other? Mercy killing?"

"Rarely, but yes."

"Good God!" Then, maybe because the entire evening had been too much, a tear rolled down her cheek.

"Don't do that," he whispered.

The next thing she knew, her face was cupped in his cool, gentle hands, and he leaned close enough to lick the tear from her cheek. It was such an intimate gesture, and it caused a thrill, a purely sexual thrill, to race through her. Her heart stuttered into a faster pace, and her breaths came more rapidly. She absolutely *ached.*

He pulled back a little, still cupping her face. His smile grew crooked. "Don't do that, either."

"What?"

"How much more can you take tonight, Yvonne?"

"What do you mean?"

His thumb brushed her damp cheek. "I told you I want you. But now I know you want me, too. I can hear your heartbeat. I can smell your pheromones."

Immediately she felt her cheeks flush. "Can I just dig a hole now?"

He chuckled quietly and brushed her hot cheeks with his thumbs again. "That blush drives me wild. And I know you can't help it. I was just teasing you."

In a flash he reappeared in the chair farthest from her. "Right now I think you're safer if I'm over here."

She clapped her hands to her cheeks, trying to remember the last time she had felt so embarrassed. She had believed she had lost the ability to blush some time ago, but around Creed she seemed to blush frequently.

Probably because of her attraction to him. And oh, it was some attraction! She wished he hadn't pulled away. She wished… She wished too much.

"Can you read my mind?" Her voice sounded thick even to her. Desire and apprehension both swamped her.

"No, that's a myth. But there's a lot I can tell from your scents, things a human couldn't consciously detect, or maybe couldn't detect at all. And from your heartbeat."

"So I'm an open book?"

He shrugged. "Your immediate emotional reactions are. But nothing else."

"Oh." She wondered how unnerving that was going to become. Right now it was merely downright embarrassing.

"Regardless," he said kindly, "given the number of shocks you've had this evening, I wouldn't trust your impulses. So I'll just keep a bit of distance and make it easier on both of us."

The way she felt right now, she wasn't sure that was a good thing. For God's sake, she didn't even care that he was a vampire. What she needed was closeness, comfort, distraction.

Which, she supposed, made him right about not trusting her impulses. With effort, she forced her thoughts away from her immediate longing. "What did Garner mean about vampires being impervious to demons?"

"That's not one hundred percent true, but it's not as easy for them to possess us."

"Why not?"

He shrugged. "Maybe because we're unnatural."

"You know, that bothers me."

"What does?"

"That you call yourself unnatural. You exist. That makes you natural, unless you can prove you emerged from a test tube concoction."

He laughed quietly. "I like that."

"Well, it's true. You exist. You guys have apparently existed for a long time?"

"There are a few still around who remember Babylon and ancient Egypt."

"Then it must be natural. But only a few that old?"

"We can die, Yvonne. We may be harder to kill, but we can die. The difference between us is that I will die a second time."

"Was the first time awful?" She immediately wished she hadn't asked, because his face shadowed and his eyes turned black. He was out of the chair so fast she didn't see him move, and she realized he was pacing only when he paused to turn.

"Can you slow down? I can't see you."

"Oh, sorry." Creed slowed to something

closer to a mortal pace. It was still almost enough to make her dizzy.

"You don't have to tell me," she said.

"No, I don't. But I suppose I will. I doubt you can imagine the rage I felt when I realized what that woman had done to me. That she had turned me into this…this monster, that I couldn't go home, that my every instinct was to prey on my fellow man. I was sickened, and furious, and I even tried to kill her. Especially when I went to my family and realized I could harm them. Especially then. So I backed away. For a while that was the only restraint I was able to manage."

"Why?"

He faced her. "Because the instincts of a newborn vampire are overpowering, the hunger is overwhelming, so overwhelming that anything as paltry as clear thinking is almost impossible. You *have* to feed. It's a hunger beyond reason, beyond thought. Then, if there's any humanity left in you, you loathe yourself."

Her heart ached for him, and the tightness in her chest kept her from speaking for a short while. "I'm so sorry. Do you still hate yourself?"

"I am what I am, and as long as I keep my self-control, I can live with it."

"Do all vampires feel that way?"

"Hell no. Some revel in their worst instincts, and justify it as being part of their nature. Some of us resist. Just never forget, Yvonne. We're predators by nature."

She nodded, thinking it over. The world was full of predators who killed to eat, including the human race. She supposed it mattered how they did it and why. "I don't like to watch a cat kill. Even lions play with their food sometimes."

"It's part of the hunt, part of the pleasure."

She suppressed a shudder, wondering if it was part of his nature, too. "What I don't like thinking about is the terror their prey must feel."

"Many of us don't terrorize our prey. It's not necessary to be sadistic."

"Do you play with them?" Because if he said they did, she didn't know if she could stand it.

He stilled. In fact he became so still that she wondered if he had turned to stone. He didn't even seem to be breathing. Finally he said, "We play a different way with our prey."

Her heart seemed to climb into her throat. She didn't know if she wanted to hear this, but at the same time she *needed* to. She had to know what Creed was before her yearning for him got her in any deeper. Tommy had taught her that bit of wisdom. "What's that?"

"Not what, but how. Shall I complete your education? Shall I truly appall you?"

"How?" She felt almost like backing away, except she was curled on the corner of the couch, and he stood between her and escape.

"We provide sexual pleasure, Yvonne. If we don't kill our prey, they spend the rest of their lives hunting for another such experience, like addicts seeking cocaine. Pleasure, not pain, is the key to our survival."

"Oh." She barely breathed the word as the air seemed to flee the room. An instinctive throbbing began between her legs, and her heart began a slow, heavy drumbeat. "How can anything be that good?"

Instantaneously, it seemed, he was there, bent over her. He leaned toward her, just enough. His lips hovered near her neck below her ear, and she could feel the whisper of his cool breath. A shiver of longing pierced her center. "I could make you want me forever. And you have no idea just how much I'd like to do that."

Now she definitely couldn't breathe. She felt as if she'd just been dumped into outer space. Every cell in her body awoke and began to throb with need.

"I want to take you to that place with me more than I've ever wanted to take any other human. But I won't. There's no future in it, Yvonne. So I'll leave you unscathed to get on with your normal life once we take care of Asmodai."

Then, before she could register more than a stir in the air, he was back across the room.

She sighed and let her head droop, closing her eyes for a few moments, waiting for the sexual tension to ease. He was right on so many levels, regardless of whether she might become addicted to him—and she found that hard to believe, but then most of this evening was hard to believe. Still, she didn't know him well, and she wasn't the sort of woman to take sex lightly. Even when she was supercharged with adrenaline, which was probably most of what was going on.

She was tired. So tired. Too much had happened, and the day was already too long. She needed sleep and wondered if she would be able to, tired or not, because she suspected that the minute she started to doze off, she'd get walloped all over again by the things that had happened.

A demon named Asmodai was interested in her for some unknown reason, and she couldn't escape the feeling that Tommy was the cause. Damn, how had she been so blind to what he must have been up to? Because it had to be Tommy.

She couldn't think of a single thing she might have done herself to draw the attention of a demon. Not one. She lived a very ordinary life, spending her days working, her evenings reading, or occasionally visiting a friend, or having one over. As lives went, hers approached the downright boring.

Until now. Something had certainly changed somewhere, somehow. Tommy and his threats were all she could think of. God, she hated to think she'd shared her life with someone who would play with dark powers. But what was she thinking? She hadn't *known* Tommy might be involved in such things, but she had no excuse when it came to her desire for Creed. And damn, she wanted him, vampire or not. How did she process *that* idiocy?

Without warning, strong arms lifted her from the couch. Startled, she reached out and wrapped her arms around Creed's neck. He made her feel as if she didn't weigh an ounce. "Creed!"

"You're tired. You need sleep. Do you want to change?"

Even that seemed like too much effort. The only things she seemed to want right now were to stay in Creed's arms and sleep. "Not really." The sweatshirt and jeans she was wearing were old, soft and comfortable.

She looked around his room as he carried her inside, taking in its paucity of furnishings. Apparently he didn't think a bedroom he enjoyed only when he was dead merited much attention. It was bare bones, the only luxury a chair and a small desk in the corner. And a small refrigerator in another corner. If there had ever been a window, it was gone.

"Are you cold?" he asked. "I can't tell."

"A little."

"Covers or should I turn the heat up?"

"Covers." She preferred snuggling into blankets.

He totally amazed her by holding her easily with one arm while he pulled the blankets back. Then he set her down gently, tugged off her shoes and pulled covers back up over her.

"I'll bring your things in here so you can get at them in the morning. Just don't open the door tomorrow, Yvonne. Please."

"I promise I won't."

He straightened, brushing his fingertips lightly against her cheek. They were so smooth, the touch so welcome, that she could have purred. "I'll put some food in here for you, too, so you don't have to starve all day. You saw the refrigerator over there?"

"Yes." God, impossible as it seemed, her eyelids were growing heavy. Sleep took her between one breath and the next.

Creed watched her sleep for a while. He hadn't watched a woman sleep since his wife, and he'd forgotten how much he had once loved to do that. He loved the soft sighs, the little murmurs, the occasional restless stirring. The defenselessness perhaps. Sleeping with someone else in the room was a mark of complete trust.

But Yvonne's scent, even in sleep, was enough to push him to the brink of lust and hunger, so he didn't watch her slumber as long as he might have. Instead he leashed himself and returned to his desk, determined to work until dawn.

Anything to escape constant awareness of the luscious package in his bed.

Except instead he found himself researching Asmodai. Or Asmodeus. He doubted he had anything on his bookshelf on the subject, but as an academic and professional researcher, he had access to libraries not available to the average web searcher.

What he found in his searches among Jewish scholars caused him to sit back in deep thought. Asmodai spent time in heaven, not hell apparently, but returned to earth to do his mischief. And Solomon had controlled him with a neck chain bearing the Tetragrammaton, the four Hebrew letters that represented the name of God.

Well, getting such a chain would be easy

enough but putting it on a demon was another matter altogether. Asmodai had been tricked before through thirst, which had caused him to drink too much wine, and thus he had fallen into a sleep that allowed the chain to be placed on him. Not a likely solution for a city where every dwelling had a water tap.

Otherwise, apparently you needed an archangel. Yeah, archangels grew on every tree.

He picked up a pencil and rapped the eraser quietly against his desktop as he pondered. The story of Asmodai and women was a rather muddy one. Much disagreement existed on whether he fell in love with them, whether he had been sent by heaven to teach a lesson in chastity by means of Sarah and Tobias, or whether he just plain lusted after some women. That he had congress with women was not in doubt, however.

He glanced toward his bedroom and felt rather sickened at what might happen to Yvonne if they didn't find a way to bind that thing. And he thought *he* was bad for her?

At least he wouldn't give her any two-headed children. Indeed, no children at all. Which in itself was hardly better than giving her a monster to bear. Every woman seemed to want children, and he couldn't offer that.

He couldn't offer her much at all. A half life, existence in the shadows, a wrenching move every decade or so. Always living on the outside, never the inside.

Maybe watching Terri and Jude in their happiness had stirred things in him he'd given up on long ago. He certainly didn't know Yvonne well enough to be worrying about what kind of future he could offer her.

No, the only thing he needed to be concerned about was protecting her from a demon and from himself.

That was more than enough to contend with.

He was deep into research when a tapping at his window alerted him. He had a terrace outside around much of his penthouse and it was a place he enjoyed on quiet nights when nothing pressed him. But hearing a tap when no one should be out there alerted him to the type of visitor he had.

In a flash he crossed the room and recognized the vampire who stood outside: Luc St. Just. He hadn't seen Luc in over fifty years, not since they had worked together to bring down a newborn vampire who held an entire city in a state of terror because she wouldn't control her appetites. The vampire who had created the newborn had been punished as well for failing to maintain control of her. Since then, he and Luc had gone their separate ways, for it was the way of vampires not to congregate for long, in order to avoid drawing attention.

He opened the sliding glass door and stepped out. Luc was fast, though. He sniffed the air. "You have food inside? I thought you didn't indulge."

"I don't. I'm helping a friend."

"Ahh." Luc, who cut a dashing figure and liked to flaunt it, backed away and leaned against the terrace wall. He always dressed elegantly, and drew the ladies' eyes with his pale blond hair and golden eyes. "Must be devilishly difficult for you."

Creed ignored that. "What are you doing here?"

"I'm on my way north. Julianne suggested I join her where the nights are very long. I heard you were here so I thought I'd say hello."

All these centuries, and Luc still had a hint

of French in his English. And Creed didn't believe this visit was *en passant.* "Nice of you."

Luc laughed. "You don't trust me, my friend."

"Do I have reason not to?"

"No. Of course not. I also heard that something ugly is trying to happen here."

Creed tensed slightly, but forced his face to remain smooth. Alliances among vampires tended to be born of necessity, not desire, and friendship was even rarer. "So it seems. Who did you hear from?"

"The whispers are everywhere. Your friend, Jude Messenger, is getting quite a reputation. I hear he had a difficult case a few months ago."

"Yes."

"And I hear something is going on now. People talk, you know. Even humans get wind of things, and we listen. Then, of course, I planned my trip so we might share a glass or two, and when I got close I smelled something." Luc's usually cheerful face darkened. "Asmodai."

"What are you talking about?"

"He tried in Marseilles five years ago, my friend. He tried. He killed my Natasha."

Creed felt an immediate pang. Natasha had been lovely, and she and Luc had seemed to be such a perfect fit. The kind of claiming that would never cause trouble. "I'm sorry, Luc. I didn't hear about it."

"You're so buried in your books I doubt you hear much, Creed. I have a score to settle. You know what I mean."

Indeed Creed did. Luc had claimed Natasha, which meant he would stop at nothing to avenge Natasha's death. Nothing. Vengeance or death would be all that would end Luc's claiming.

And Creed could well see the problems that might be caused by an unhinged vampire hunting Asmodai. But first some questions. "You're saying he got through? How? And how did you send him back?"

Luc shrugged. "I don't have answers, my friend. But I want them now."

"Let me call Jude," Creed said, pulling out his cell. "You can't do this alone. What's more, you can't just waltz into this and create havoc. There are other lives at stake, Luc."

"I know that. You think I care?"

In an instant, Creed turned predatory. Gone

was the veneer he wore. He snarled and half crouched. His voice deepened, no longer sounding human. "Listen to me, Luc. If you do anything that causes harm to Jude and his people, or to that woman I'm protecting, I'll take you out myself."

Luc's eyes turned black, but he didn't snarl back, or threaten. "I don't want to hurt you or Jude. But I'll do what I must."

Before Creed could say another word, Luc disappeared over the edge of the terrace wall. By the time Creed gathered himself, he was certain that Luc had vanished into the shadows.

At once he called Jude, tension tightening his nerves until they felt like steel cables.

This was bad news indeed, and the main focus of his concern was Yvonne, sleeping so innocently in his bed. Now he had to protect her not only against a demon, but against a maddened vampire.

And he was damned if he knew which might be worse.

From somewhere just outside of time, Asmodai watched, pleased. The pieces in this little game had just come together. Luc could act against the other two undead, and create the opening it needed. Satisfied that it had created a volatile mix, it turned its attention to other amusements. For now.

Chapter 6

Yvonne awoke at nearly ten the next morning. The digital clock on the bedside table cast a red glow through the room. At least she thought it was morning. It had to be because she couldn't have slept through until the following night. Sitting up, she reached around for the lamp she remembered being beside her. When she flicked it on, it provided minimal illumination.

The room was utterly silent except for her own movements. So silent she thought she must be alone. But when she rolled over to look, she saw Creed stretched out on the floor, fully clothed, flat on his back. He appeared to be sleeping.

She held her breath, listening, and realized he truly wasn't breathing.

So it was all true. It hadn't been a crazy dream.

Quietly, although she didn't know why she felt the need for stealth, she climbed out of bed and crept over to him. When she knelt beside him, she put her ear to his lips.

Definitely not breathing. Then she rested her hand over his heart and waited. No heartbeat. None.

She jerked back, partly because she felt she was trespassing, and partly because the reality of her situation came home to her again.

It was real. All of it.

A shuddering sigh escaped her, and she continued to kneel beside him, absorbing the realities she hadn't fully connected with the night before.

Last night she had accepted everything, but now the truth of it hit, and it hit hard. What had she been thinking last night?

Nothing, evidently. Everything had seemed so casual and so muffled that at some level nothing had penetrated. Yes, she'd experienced that *thing* in her apartment. Yes, she'd seen Creed move so fast he seemed to vanish and reappear, she'd watched him drink blood, she'd seen his eyes turn to chips of black coal.

But something had kept the reality of it all from coming home.

Now, suddenly shaking like a leaf in a hurricane, she wanted to deny it all, to cram reality back into its familiar box and lock out all the things that belonged in fantasy, not reality. She wanted to go back to the relative safety of the world she had lived in before Creed, before that god-awful feeling in her apartment. A world where things like this only happened in the pages of a book.

But lying before her on the floor was a man who, for all intents and purposes, was dead. She felt body-slammed as last night rushed home at last to her brain and her emotions. Gasping for breath, she pushed herself back on her hands and knees away from him.

It was true. All of it was *true.* And she could no more escape from that knowledge than she could return to her apartment and resume a normal life.

Shock lifted its hazy veil and left her with a world forever changed. For once, with the evidence lying right in front of her, denial wasn't going to work.

She could run away right now. Every cell in her body wanted to do exactly that. But she vividly remembered his warning not to open the door. He had trusted her, and not even fear could make her betray that trust.

But, God, with her brain running in crazy, pointless circles like a hamster in a wheel, unable to find a place to stop and rest in this new world, she didn't know how she was going to handle this.

A vampire. For real.

She slid away even farther until her back was to the wall. An internal earthquake rattled her, worse even than when she had learned Tommy was cheating. Cheating, at least, fit into things that happened in the real world. But not vampires. Most definitely not.

Nor did demons, actually, and certainly not the prince of them. Yet according to someone her friend Detective Pat Matthews trusted, she was facing exactly that.

So what, she asked herself, was worse?

Being hunted by a demon or protected by a vampire?

Neither question seemed to make sense. They sounded ridiculous, ludicrous, even within the private confines of her own mind.

Finally she put her head in her hands and waited, just waited. So much adrenaline would not help her think. Not at all.

Not that she felt afraid of him. Maybe she should. Maybe it would be wise. But he'd been honest with her, and she trusted him to be a man of his word.

She ought to know better than that, given Tommy, but Creed struck her as a far better man. He'd given her the truth, after all, even when it could have caused him serious problems.

Curious, she crept close again and reached out to touch his cheek. Smooth. Cool. Room temperature, as he'd said, but not chilly. And not even the tiniest bit of evidence of beard growth. She snatched her hand back in surprise, then slowly reached out again. Definitely no beard stubble. Yet his skin still felt smooth and supple. Alive even though he evidently was not. How weird was that?

Inevitably, she took the opportunity to drink him in with her eyes. He was a very handsome man, with patrician features and a firm jaw. The kind of face that would always draw a woman's eye. When he was awake, the golden color of his eyes was beautiful. The black not so much. She needed to ask him why his eyes changed like that, and when.

But first she needed to absorb all the shocks. To just let it all roll through her until it found a place to settle.

Finally she drew back to the table where he'd set her computer, another lamp and beside it her suitcase. To her surprise, she discovered he'd left the coffeemaker for her, plugged in and ready to brew a pot. She switched it on, then turned so she could watch him again.

Reason and instinct warred for a while, but finally, being a realist, she had to admit that the things she had seen and experienced could have no other explanation than the one he'd given her: that he was a vampire. She could still question whether a demon was stalking her, but she couldn't question what she'd seen with her own eyes.

So okay, she needed to knit together a new

version of reality, and as she sat there sipping coffee, she realized it really wasn't that difficult. There was so much about the world that was still unknown. Why not vampires?

And if vampires were mostly like Creed and Jude, why should she panic? Really. In fact, even if most vampires weren't like Creed and Jude, what did it matter? They were the only vampires she knew.

She continued to stare at Creed, vaguely aware that she was growing hungry, but unable to stop looking. God, she felt as if her interest in him was evolving into a craving. How could that be? For heaven's sake, he was *undead*. But even just looking at him was enough to make her pulse pound a little, and a hard ache to occur between her legs.

Oh, she'd been so intelligent and bright last night, saying he must be natural or he wouldn't exist. And it was true. But at some level she didn't quite believe that. Or did she?

Sighing, giving up the internal arguments at last, she resigned herself to the fact that no amount of reasoning or emotion would change the basic facts: Creed appeared to be exactly what he said he was, and regardless of what he was, she wanted him with a kind of longing she'd never really felt before. Not even for Tommy.

"Don't be stupid," she said aloud. Creed never stirred. So okay, he was dead. Undead. Whatever. And she *was* being stupid because what did she know about vampires except silly stories from myth and novels? Evidently a lot of what she thought she knew was wrong.

What was more, he had showed her the ultimate trust. There he lay, completely helpless, and he'd shared his room with her. He'd trusted her not to take advantage of his vulnerability in his death sleep, or whatever it was. Because even though he said he could wake up if necessary, she suspected there were a whole lot of terrible things she could do to him that he couldn't protect himself from quickly enough… like opening the bedroom door and letting in the sunlight.

His trust cracked through the last of her fear. How could she fear someone who had put his life in her hands?

Eventually, after her shower and change, she faced the refrigerator. On top of it sat some boxes of crackers, a few plates and flatware. She hesitated, however, when it came to opening the small fridge. She knew most of what she would find in there: bags of blood. Why that should make her hesitate after watching Creed drink it, she didn't know. For the first time she saw the biohazard container tucked in beside it. That seemed curious.

Finally she opened the refrigerator door and felt surprised that it wasn't full of bags of blood. In fact, there were only three in there. The rest of the space was filled with leftovers from last night's meal and the unopened cheese that had been in his kitchen the day before.

After a moment of hesitation, she decided on cheese and crackers; she could eat the leftovers later.

It was odd to spend the day in a dark room, with only a little lamplight, but far from as difficult or unnerving as she had initially expected. In fact, all that happened was that with a choice between sitting in boredom or working, she got a lot of work done.

Time passed almost unnoticed, between being busy and having no visual cues other than the clock. She wound up being startled when she heard a gasp. She had become so absorbed in her writing that she had forgotten she was not alone.

Turning, she saw Creed, his eyes open. His face appeared twisted, but quickly smoothed out. An instant later he was on his feet. Evidently it surprised him a bit to awaken and discover he wasn't alone, because at first he crouched, as if ready for a fight.

Then he straightened and gave her a smile. "Good evening."

"That looked like it hurt."

"Resurrection always hurts. Are you tired of this room?"

"I could be."

"Has it been an awful day?"

"Actually not. It's amazing how much writing I can do when there aren't any distractions."

A low laugh escaped him. "My feeling about most nights, usually."

He took a few minutes in the bath to clean up. She heard the shower run, heard the sink tap. The sounds of things being moved.

Amazingly intimate sounds, given that there was a closed door between them. She closed her computer after saving her work and waited. Not long: he moved fast.

He emerged dressed in fresh clothes, another version of black, this time a bulky sweater and slacks.

"Do you always wear black?"

He paused as he slipped his feet into shoes. "Usually. It makes it easier to blend with the shadows." He finished donning his shoes and went to open the bedroom door. "Jude and Terri should be here soon. I asked Terri to bring a decent meal for you."

"Have they found out something?"

"No, I don't think so. But we've developed a complication."

Her heart jammed. "We don't already have enough complications?"

"Apparently not. But I'll tell you about it over dinner. Then we can discuss everything we know, and everything we don't know."

"The everything we don't know is the part that worries me most."

He opened the bedroom door, and for the first time she realized it had an unusual lock. As he pressed the bar handle, she could hear three dead bolts snap open, one after another.

He threw the door wide, revealing the twilit city through the windows beyond.

Then he surprised her. Instead of leaving the room, he came to kneel in front of her. Reaching out, he touched her cheek. His voice grew husky. "You drive me mad. This room is full of your scent now. Such a desirable scent."

Her heart skipped to a faster rhythm. Was he going to kiss her? She actually found herself tensing with hope that he would.

"You can leave," he said. "You can walk out of this room. Do you believe me?"

She did. Surprisingly, she definitely believed she could. But she didn't move except to nod. Instead she waited, fascinated, yearning, ignoring every sensible thought that tried to pop into her head.

Moving so slowly that she could not mistake what was coming, so slowly that she had plenty of time to avert it, he leaned toward her and kissed her.

The touch of his cool lips electrified her. Shocks zinged throughout her entire body. It was a light kiss, a gentle touching of lips, but she couldn't leave it there. No. Needing so much more, she twined her arms around his neck, opening her entire body to any touch he might choose to give her. For an instant she felt him deepen the kiss. His hand brushed over her breast, unleashing a new aching wave of longing. A surge of triumph slammed her. In that moment, she wanted him beyond thought and reason, beyond any desire she had ever felt in her life.

And for a little while, he seemed about ready to give it to her. His hand kneaded her breast to aching fullness, through the layers of cloth his thumb brushed her nipple until she gasped and her hips, of their own accord, tilted toward him. She parted her legs, making room for him, needing him to touch her there, needing it with such depth and strength that she couldn't think of anything else. Had he leaned toward her, she would have welcomed him and made herself his.

Then he was gone.

Her eyes, now heavy-lidded with passion, had to search to discover he stood in the doorway.

"I shouldn't have done that."

"Why not?"

"One should never taste forbidden fruit." Then he turned and vanished.

Disappointment slammed her so hard she doubled over.

Much more of this, Creed thought, and he was going to turn into the kind of monster he loathed. Being locked up with a woman who aroused his every instinct and hunger to raging levels was turning into a test he might well fail.

He took no comfort in the fact that he had just pulled away when his entire nature was screaming for him to drink, to have sex. No mortal could understand the extremity of craving a vampire felt for those things.

He was like a man who had spent days in a desert without any water and at last had caught sight of an oasis. He had to keep reminding himself that that oasis was merely a mirage, that Yvonne was simply curious and attracted, just an illusion that would flit away as soon as the danger was past.

But his thirst for her couldn't be slaked by reminders of reality. No, the mirage drew him as powerfully as if it were real.

He stood staring out over the darkening city

without seeing it, because all he could notice were Yvonne's scents, powerful even at this distance, even though she had not yet emerged from the bedroom.

Trial by fire, he thought with bitter amusement. Atoning in these hours for every sin he'd ever committed. He doubted hell itself could offer worse torment than self-denial of something so essential and needed.

Much more of this, and he might well need a straitjacket.

"Creed?"

Reluctantly he turned to see her standing in the open doorway of his bedroom. "Yes?"

"Why?"

"Why what?"

"Why am I forbidden fruit?"

Hell. He really didn't want to discuss this with her, and he'd already tried to explain once. It was hard enough to contain all this within himself.

"Because I'm dangerous to you," he said flatly. "Because I could hurt you without meaning to."

"How?"

He swore quietly and turned his back to her.

Bad enough he had to deal with her enticing scents without seeing her, as well. "Because, if I were to forget myself, I could make you crave me forever. I told you that."

"Isn't that *my* problem?"

He swung around, nearly glaring. "You don't get it, Yvonne. You don't begin to get it. Look at me. As near as I can tell, I have no purpose but to seduce and drink. Everything about me is designed to make you want me. And if I drink from you sufficiently, what you feel now will pale by comparison. I've seen humans become totally consumed by the need to repeat the experience of making love with a vampire, of being drunk from by a vampire. They might as well be crack addicts."

"Oh." Her voice was small.

"I know you want me. I want you, too. And the pull I'm feeling toward you is so strong, so unusually strong, that I can't trust myself to stop soon enough if I start."

"I see."

He was certain she didn't, but he sure as hell didn't know how to make her see when the reality was so far from her experience.

She had no idea, of course, that he could

truly feel her desire for him almost as strongly as he could feel his own. That her scents, her heartbeat—audible even at this distance—made him feel her yearning, and that there was no more powerful aphrodisiac in the world.

Or that resisting her might require more willpower than he could muster.

He was actually relieved when his doorbell rang and even more relieved when he opened it and found not just Jude but also Terri, Chloe and Garner.

Terri breezed in first, carrying a large bag from a restaurant, followed by Chloe who winked at him as if she knew *exactly* what kind of hell he was going through and actually had the cheek to think it was cool. She, too, carried a large restaurant bag.

Terri and Chloe went about setting a table for the four humans, with some help from Yvonne who seemed glad to be surrounded by some other females, especially human ones. Not that he could blame her. After his warning, maybe she was beginning to realize she might not be able to trust him completely. And much as it pained him to make her feel that way, it was still true. If he couldn't trust *himself,* then it was dangerous for her to trust. God, sometimes he hated himself!

When everyone had gathered around the table Creed carried two armchairs closer for him and Jude. He saw Yvonne's eyes widen at the sight of him carrying those chairs, one in each hand, as if they were made of paper.

Good, let her think about what that might mean. He needed her to pull away before his self-control lost the battle against instinctive drives. A little avoidance from the morsel would be welcome at this point.

Of course, the aromas of the food the humans were eating hardly affected him. What affected him was being so close to four humans each of whom smelled like a meal to a starving man. He smothered a sigh and tried to focus on the issues.

"Okay," Garner said. "I found a couple of people who are possessed. I found hints of the same stench from Yvonne's apartment around them, but just faint traces. My guess is that he's being cagey for the moment. Trying not to leave too much of a trail."

"It's Asmodai for certain," Creed announced. "Luc St. Just recognized the stench, and he would know."

"Ah, Luc," said Jude. "Another major headache."

Garner spoke. "I'm not the only one?"

Jude looked at Garner from the corner of his eye.

Garner waved a hand. "Can you blame me for being glad I'm not the only thorn in your side?"

Jude sighed.

Yvonne stirred. "Who is Luc and why is he a problem?"

"Luc," Creed explained, "is another vampire. He showed up here last night. He'd gotten wind of Asmodai, and he's out for revenge."

"Why?"

Creed hesitated. In mixed company, explaining a claiming was difficult. Hell, it was difficult to discuss even among vampires, since it was something they preferred not to think about. He decided the condensed version was safest. "Asmodai killed his mate five years ago."

"Natasha," Jude said, his face darkening. "She was a delight."

"Yes, she was. And Luc said he doesn't care what it costs, even in terms of lives, but he will take his revenge."

"Great," said Garner. "You have me out there hunting for a demon who can kill even vampires? Uh, I don't think so!"

"Oh, hush," Chloe snapped, slapping at his arm. "You're the one who's been driving Jude and me nuts for the past two years insisting that you're good enough to work with us."

"Nobody said anything about a demon even you vampires can't protect me from."

"Are you a demon hunter or not?"

Garner glared at her.

"Chicken," said Chloe, and sniffed.

"I'm not a chicken. But Asmodai?" Garner's voice almost reached a squeak on the name. A look from Jude silenced him.

Creed wished Yvonne would do more than pick at her food, a serving of chicken marsala. She needed to keep her strength up. Humans weren't like vampires: they couldn't go several days without eating and not suffer for it. But he didn't know how to encourage her to eat.

Finally, Creed leaned toward her, just an inch

or two. "Look how many are gathered here to fight this thing. You're not alone."

Her green eyes met his, hinting at fear, but not so much that it quelled her spark. "I'm grateful to everyone. I realize you're all fighting this. But I need to be able to do *something*. I can't impose on you forever. Sometimes I even have to go out. So it would great if I could help get rid of this thing. Instead I feel a bit like bait dangling in the wind. I'd rather take action."

"Action will have to wait," Jude said. "We need to find the others who are being pulled in to create the pentagram. And we need to find a way to deal with Luc before he makes a mess."

"Luc will be back," Creed said with certainty. "He knows I'm aware of Asmodai. He's got to know he can't deal with this solo."

Chloe spoke. "Then why didn't he listen to you last night?"

"Because Luc has quite a temper. My guess would be the scent of Asmodai infuriated him. He'll calm down enough to think. He may have already. But we're dealing with…" He stopped himself, unwilling to get into claiming. He suspected Chloe knew about it, but he wasn't sure about Garner, and then there was Yvonne.

Although maybe she needed to know so she'd protect herself by backing away from him.

But Jude laid it out there. "We're dealing with a claiming," he said flatly.

Terri gasped. Chloe's eyes grew huge. The question was inevitable now.

Garner barely started to inhale before Jude said, "Shut up, Garner. Yvonne, Creed will explain to you later. Let's move on."

"Move on?" Chloe asked incredulously. "This changes everything." She looked from Jude to Creed. "Are you *sure* he'll control himself? Because if he arrives helter-skelter in the midst of a ritual, there's no telling what might be unleashed. If Jude hasn't warned you about that yet, let me do it. He's sure warned *me* enough times."

"I'll talk to him," Creed replied. He could promise no more than that. "I think he'll realize that he's more likely to get what he wants if he works *with* us. Especially since he seems to have no idea how Asmodai emerged five years ago, or what sent him back afterward. What's he going to do on his own?"

"Why do people always tell me to shut up?" Garner complained. "I'm the one out there hunting these things. If there's a problem I need to know."

Jude frowned. "All you need to know is to stay out of the way of Luc St. Just. And tell him nothing."

"Oh." Garner wagged his head. "Since when has it been possible not to answer a vampire's questions?"

"Since you got some backbone?" Chloe suggested.

"You never have any trouble ignoring me," Jude reminded him.

"You've never tried to vamp me."

"Oh, yes, I have. Every time I tell you not to do something. It's worked so splendidly, hasn't it?"

Creed saw Yvonne raise her hand to cover her mouth, and he was relieved to see amusement dancing around her eyes.

Terri outright giggled, and Garner shot her a look. "You, too?" he asked. "Why does everyone think I'm a joke?"

"Not a joke, Garner," Terri assured him. "Honestly. You're just…cute."

Garner settled back, clearly not certain how

to take that. "*Puppies* are cute," he grumbled finally.

"Exactly, pup," Jude said. "Enjoy it while it lasts. Okay, so we have two possessed identified?"

"There may be a third one," Garner answered. "I couldn't get close enough to be sure today. But I'll start again in a few hours. And Terri let me check the morgue today. Your guess was right. That person who was killed the other night appears to have died during an attempted possession by you-know-who."

Silence fell around the table. Creed could smell the fear that pierced Yvonne at this news and he wished he had some comfort to offer. Then he sighed, acknowledging that any comfort at this point would be specious anyway. Hell, he was frightened himself, for her. What had started as a job had grown into something that had definitely begun to involve him at a personal level. A very personal level.

So much for all the defenses he thought he'd built.

Jude spoke. "An additional assignment, Garner. I want you to try to find Yvonne's former boyfriend. Get the necessary information from her when we're done here. All right then. We have the beginnings of the circle. Once we have them all…" He trailed off.

"Once we have them all," Creed said, though he was well aware that Jude, and not he, was the expert here, "we need to make sure they come together at a time and place of *our* choosing." Easier said than done, of course.

Jude nodded. "I agree, though it won't be easy. I need to give some thought to that. There may be a way. Hell, there *has* to be a way, because we definitely need the advantage. Anything else?"

"That last time Asmodai was bound, it was done by chaining the Tetragrammaton around his neck. Getting that on him is not going to be easy, I suspect. Assuming we can get one made in time."

Then Creed sat back, frowning thoughtfully. "But I may know exactly where to get one. I seem to remember one being mentioned, one on a blackened chain…" He trailed off then suddenly smiled. "I do think my dear friend Avi Herschel has a story he needs to tell me."

Jude stirred. "Just remember, Creed. You've got to watch Yvonne. Don't forget, Luc may be a threat to her, too."

Yvonne stiffened, but didn't ask the obvious. Instead she appeared to force herself to eat a few bites of her chicken. Why did he think that she was saving up a whole lot of unpleasant questions for later?

Probably because he knew damn well she wasn't incurious by nature. Yes, she'd ask. He just hoped he'd provide acceptable answers.

Because, at heart, he wasn't sure just how much of his dark, hidden world he wanted to display to her. What if she was horrified? Worse, what if she wasn't?

There was evidently no good answer to the question of Yvonne Depuis and his hunger for her.

So he sat there, listening as the discussion lightened to ordinary things, and wondered if a vampire could go insane, short of losing the object of a claiming.

He'd spent the better part of a century avoiding the line he was treading here with Yvonne.

A very narrow, very dangerous line. One he might trip over at any instant.

Yes, he was crazy. To what degree only time would tell.

It paid some attention now, taking care not to draw close enough for the hunter to smell it. It listened, but could make out very little of what was said. Not that it mattered.

It had drawn the undead one here, the one who called himself Luc. That one would destroy all the plans these others were making. That was what it had called him here to do.

Chapter 7

As the meal finished up, Chloe dragged Garner into the kitchenette to wash dishes. Creed and Jude stepped outside onto the terrace as if it were not a frigid autumn night. Terri gave a small jerk of her head to Yvonne and led her back into the empty spare bedroom.

They sat cross-legged on the carpeted floor.

"I'm going to be nosy," Terri said.

"Be my guest. If I get annoyed, I'll tell you."

"Good. You're attracted to Creed, aren't you?"

Yvonne hesitated, then nodded. "I have been since I first saw him. And since my last boyfriend cheated on me, I don't want to be attracted."

Terri winced. "Ouch!"

"Yeah. For six of the eight months we were together."

"How did you find out?"

"The other girlfriend found out about me somehow and called me."

"Even more fun."

"Well, she dumped him, too."

Terri laughed quietly. "Good."

"But you didn't want to talk about that."

Terri hesitated. "No. It's just that…well, Creed is struggling, Yvonne. He's trying very hard to tamp down his natural instincts around you. From what I can tell, it's not just a passing fancy he's feeling. It's something stronger."

"He kind of said that. I wasn't sure what he meant, though." Yvonne leaned back against the wall, waiting to hear what Terri might have to say.

"Jude," Terri said, "will cheerfully tell you I nearly drove him insane. And honestly, I didn't really understand. I mean, it seems so simple to just tell yourself that you can't have someone.

I've done it more than once when I had a crush of some kind."

"Are you saying it's different for vampires?"

"Very different." Terri tipped her head to one side. "Chloe read me the riot act one night. She told me that Jude was like someone who'd been drinking rotgut wine and all of a sudden a bottle of the finest champagne was in reach. And I was the champagne."

Yvonne felt a little shock, a surprisingly pleasant one. And with it a throbbing hint of her desire. "Are you trying to warn me away?"

"Actually no. I'm just trying to tell you what you're up against. I love Jude dearly. Do you feel any attraction to him?"

Yvonne gasped. "Jude? No! Oh, I wouldn't want you to think that. Absolutely not. Did I do something?"

Terri shook her head quickly. "Not at all. It's just that vampires can cause a fascination in some people. They don't do it consciously, it just is. And one of the things that convinced Jude I was attracted to *him* and not his being a vampire was that I didn't feel the same attraction to Creed."

"Oh. Oh! I see. I hadn't even thought of that."

But how would she? All she knew about vampires was from the movies, much of which was apparently wrong, and the few things Creed had told her. "I'm obviously uneducated."

Terri laughed. "Most of us are until we meet a vampire who'll tell us the truth. No, I just wanted you to be aware of the possibility of fascination. But if you don't feel it for Jude as well, then that's not it. So how *do* you feel about Creed?"

"Curious. Drawn. I like him." More than that she honestly couldn't say, even if her body and emotions felt more strongly. She had to keep reminding herself that she hardly knew Creed, certainly not enough to feel more than the most basic of attractions. "But your description of being a bottle of champagne… Do you mean that as food?"

"Partly. They can drink from us without harming us. But they're so reluctant to do it. At least these two. They really have drawn a moral line in the sand. Which makes it all very difficult for them now, because their cravings are much stronger than we can imagine. It's not like wanting a bowl of ice cream. It's wanting something you need to survive. Like water."

Yvonne's closest experience had been a summer when she'd ignored the heat to play basketball with some girlfriends. When she got home she had drunk a full gallon of water, and wanted more. That had been the thirstiest she had ever been, and she well remembered exactly how good that water had tasted to her. "Creed said something about everything being more intense now for him."

"It is. Anyway, I couldn't hide my attraction from Jude, and you probably can't hide yours from Creed. Just… I guess what I'm trying to say is, be sure what you want. Because there's so much more involved than you and I can fully understand. Take me, for example. I had no idea the agony I caused Jude when I suggested I pay him for his services with my blood."

"You actually did that?" Amazement filled Yvonne. For all she felt attracted to Creed, she had never even considered the possibility of giving him her blood.

"Yeah, I did that. I had no idea how rough I kept making it for him to maintain his self-control. I thought, well, if he didn't want my money, maybe he'd take my blood." Terri shook her head. "He kept trying to make me go away.

Tried to shock me or horrify me so I'd just move on. And I kept right on coming back."

"Creed hasn't tried to drive me away. He just stays as far from me as possible."

"Creed's in a tough situation. He's protecting you. It's not like he can tell you to get lost."

Yvonne's heart plummeted. God, she hadn't even thought of that. Her very presence was a severe trial, evidently, and he couldn't tell her to go away. It sickened her to think what he might be enduring to keep her safe from Asmodai. She didn't want anyone to suffer like that. But what alternative did she have? He wouldn't even let her stay on her own in the daytime.

She looked down, searching for solutions and finding none. If he wouldn't let her out of his sight, she was helpless. Helpless to be anything but an unending, painful temptation.

"This is awful," she said finally, her chest tight with emotion. "Just awful."

"No, it's just what is. If Creed couldn't handle it, he would tell Jude."

"Maybe." She wasn't at all sure of that. In fact, she clearly recalled that Creed hadn't volunteered for the job of protector; Jude had designated him. So it was entirely possible he didn't want to do this at all.

She sighed, but when Terri questioned her, she just shook her head. How could she explain that she felt sick at heart thinking she was a burden Creed didn't want, one that might be causing him plenty of discomfort? She hardly knew the man. She shouldn't care that much.

But she did. And it made her a little ill.

And in her mind, she heard echoes of her mother telling her what a burden she was, how hard it was to raise a child without help, how much she had to give up in order to support Yvonne. Yvonne had reacted by becoming totally self-sufficient, refusing to lean on anyone for anything.

Now here she was, leaning again. A burden again. Her stomach flipped and something inside her turned bleak and cold.

"Yvonne?"

She looked up and saw concern in Terri's pretty face. "I'm fine."

"No, you're not and it's my fault. What did I say?"

"Nothing that isn't true. I'll try to be careful. I wouldn't want to make it harder on Creed."

Indeed, if she could, she was going to find a way not to be a burden at all. Starting with her first job at sixteen, when she'd thrown her first paycheck down on the kitchen table and told her mother to take it, it had been a policy she had followed religiously. Need no one. Rely on no one. Take from no one. Except for that small slip with Tommy, she'd adhered to that credo. In the end, Tommy had given her nothing he hadn't been prepared to give any attractive woman who had crossed his path.

There was a lesson in that.

Hiring Jude had been one thing. Living with Creed like a leech was another.

She felt a stiffening in her spine and knew she was going to find a way to take herself off Creed's hands. Until then she would remain as invisible and as much out of the way as she possibly could.

Creed noted her withdrawal as soon as they were alone again. Hyperaware as he was, acutely as sensitive as he was, he could tell to the millimeter how far she was from him. For two days now her distance had been minimal, something he had chosen more than she. Now he heard it, smelled it, saw it: she was staying as far from him as she could.

Of course. The reality of what he was had finally sunk in. He'd been expecting it. Sooner or later, despite what she had so far claimed, she had been bound to realize that he was a monster, so unnatural that his existence flew in the face of everything known about biology.

He was so "other" that he was scarcely to be tolerated. So alien he might as well have come from Zeta Reticuli.

He was fully aware of the irony, of course. Just a little while ago he had wished she would pull back a bit to make it easier on him. Now she had, and it hurt.

He watched her from across the room, noting the way she was trying not to look at him, the way she seemed to be hunching in on herself.

He didn't know what was harder to endure: her withdrawal or her delicious scent. Finally he decided he'd had enough.

"I'm going to step out onto the terrace for a breath of air." A cleansing breath of night air to escape her maddening scent for just a few minutes. Just long enough to batter down an unwanted tangle of emotions and cravings.

But he stayed out longer than a couple of minutes. The past couple of days had thrown him off stride, between Yvonne and Asmodai, and he felt a deep need to find some kind of internal balance, to settle things within himself as they had been mostly settled before Yvonne. In his own way he'd found contentment and acceptance with his mostly solitary existence, leavened by his friendship with Jude. He'd always been an introvert anyway, a man more accustomed to the reaches of his mind.

Becoming a vampire had changed all that, making him aware that he was a being with needs that had little to do with the mind, that he couldn't live in an ivory tower above the fray, that he was most definitely part of the fray.

Yet with time and determination, he'd managed to achieve some of that ivory-tower isolation again, burying himself in work, learning to love solitude in the night. Until Yvonne.

Yvonne had reminded him once again that even in his hideaway he still had wants and needs that had little to do with his brain, and much to do with his body and instincts.

She had awakened his slumbering nature,

and for her sake as well as his own, he needed to get a grip.

He thought he heard a small sound and turned to look into the apartment. He saw what he saw only because he was a vampire. Human eyes could have seen nothing except that his hall door was open.

Luc St. Just, moving a little slower because of his burden, was carrying Yvonne out of the apartment.

Instant rage filled Creed.

He needed to pause just long enough to pull open the sliding door and then he was off, following Yvonne's scent as surely as if she had left a trail glowing in the air.

Another sniff in the hallway beyond his open door and he knew St. Just had gone for the stairs. Of course. The elevator would slow him down.

Creed took off at lightning speed, his only advantage that he was unburdened, and it was not much of an advantage.

He caught a glimpse of St. Just whirling around the stairwell three floors below him. He didn't hesitate. He leaped over the railing at once and dropped like a stone, counting on catlike mobility and reflexes to allow him to catch a railing farther down.

But St. Just had the same idea, and leaped, too, risking Yvonne's life, though not his own.

Desperation filled Creed. He let go of the railing he had caught and dropped all the way to the garage level. The impact hardly jarred him. He straightened in time to see the door into the parking garage start to swing shut. He caught it and raced through it so fast he wouldn't even register as a blur to mortal eyes.

He could only think about how terrified Yvonne must feel, caught in the unbreakable grip of a strange vampire, moving at speeds so fast she wouldn't even be able to see.

"St. Just!"

Creed called out as he raced toward the other vampire, his voice taking on the timbre of the lethal hunter he seldom allowed himself to become.

St. Just stopped and turned to face him, Yvonne in his arms.

"Stay back, Creed, or I'll snap her in two."

Yvonne appeared confused and panic-stricken. Creed felt his heart hardening with hatred. All of a sudden she flailed, and Creed's heart stopped.

"Yvonne, don't fight. Play dead!"

She looked wildly at him, but obeyed, thank God, going as limp and still as she possibly could given the terror that had to be ripping through her. A terror he smelled, and knew St. Just must smell. Aphrodisiacal, tempting, taunting fear. A black wave of self-loathing raced through Creed as he registered his own response, and knew Luc must be responding in the same way.

Yvonne smelled like prey, and every vampiric instinct would be awakened in St. Just. Creed hovered on the cusp of terror for her. One false move and she might be bitten.

"Luc, let her go. She's done nothing to you."

"She's the bait. You think I wasn't listening?"

The conversation with Jude on the terrace after dinner. Apparently Luc had been listening to at least part of it. He didn't know whether to damn their incaution, or damn Luc more.

He battered down his fury, knowing he needed his mind right now. Physically he and Luc were fairly well matched, so his only edge would be to think clearly, because Luc was in the grip of deep-seated drives and would be amenable to reason only if it served his ends. Right now he was thinking only one thing: to get to Asmodai. At this point he would only agree with something that dangled that promise before him.

"Asmodai isn't ready to emerge," he told Luc. "We're looking for his circle, but it's not completely formed yet."

"But he wants this one. He'll come for her."

"And just how much do you think you'll be able to do all on your own, Luc? How much? He killed Natasha. What makes you think you can face him alone?"

"I don't care what he does to me."

That was the problem. Luc would get his vengeance or die trying. Beyond that he could not think or see.

"If you harm that woman, you'll have no bait."

That finally caused a flicker of awareness to enter Luc's wild, black eyes. Creed seized on it. "Let her go, Luc. You know you can't harm her or you'll be back at square one. Just let her go and we'll figure out some way to have you join us in our plan. You know we stand a better chance than you'll stand alone."

"I want him!" The words came out of Luc in a deafening, pained roar.

"I know you do. We'll find a way to help you. But you've got to let the human go. She's our only real link."

He could tell he wasn't getting through. Luc jumped back a step, still clutching Yvonne. "I need her. He wants her, so I need her. You're not going to take her from me."

"I didn't say that. I said we could cooperate. The three of us will stand a better chance than you alone. But one thing is certain, if you harm that woman you'll have no way to draw him."

Luc emitted a growl, so deep and loud it sounded like a lion. At the sound, Yvonne struggled again, drawing Luc's attention.

Creed stopped breathing, his every muscle tightening in preparation to spring.

"I could make her mine," Luc growled. "I could make her mine forever. She'd stay with me then of her own free will."

Yvonne froze. Black fear and loathing beyond measure filled Creed at that threat. He *had* to figure out how he could attack without hurting her. But he knew the instant he sprang, Luc could kill her. Humans were so fragile in the grip of a vampire.

"Don't do that," Creed said, forcing his voice to sound calm even though he was ready to tear this entire building to the ground. "If you do that, he may no longer want her."

"You don't know that."

"I know he chose her. And that tells me what he wants. He certainly didn't choose some vampire's toy."

Luc unleashed another deafening roar. Then he crouched, Yvonne still in his arms, and Creed steadied himself, waiting for the spring, knowing it might be his last chance to save Yvonne.

After the barest instant of hesitation, Luc flung Yvonne away. It was all Creed could do not to wince as he watched her fly like a rag doll. She was a human, so frail, so easy to harm. Fear for her fueled his rage at Luc. When he spoke it was between his teeth.

"You better not have harmed her."

Luc crouched again, snarling. "You get in my way, Creed. You should know better."

"You're the one who should know better."

But he, too, crouched, ready to spring. In the balance hung Yvonne's life. He couldn't afford to lose this confrontation for that reason alone.

Luc shifted. Creed braced. Never had he been so acutely aware that he knew absolutely nothing about fighting.

Luc sprang with blinding speed. The impact nearly knocked Creed over. Creed fought for balance even as he grabbed Luc, knowing that one of them was going to die if they battled. Strength pounded into his muscles, strength he seldom allowed himself to use.

The only way to end it would be to rip Luc's head off, and he didn't have purchase. He was fighting arms as steely as his own, being kicked by feet as powerful as his own. Pain, so seldom felt, ripped through him.

Taking a chance, he overbalanced and kicked one of Luc's legs from beneath him. At once they tumbled onto the concrete.

For an instant he was on top. He tried to squeeze Luc between his legs, felt the power of opposition. He reached for Luc's head, desperate to put an end to this now. For Yvonne's sake. At once Luc batted his arms away.

He felt ragged pain across his chest, felt himself rolling, then almost before he registered it, he heard the wind of Luc's movement.

He leaped up immediately, half expecting an attack from behind, but none came. He lifted his head and sniffed the oily, exhaust-laden air. Luc had left.

Ignoring the pain that raked his chest, he sped to Yvonne's side, kneeling beside her. Her eyes were open, and for an instant dread pierced his heart. She looked so lifeless!

But then she whispered, "Is he gone?"

Creed was past rationalizing anything, including his own behavior. With extreme care, making sure she didn't cry out at any movement, he scooped her up gently in his arms. "Let's get back to my place. Then we'll see if you need a doctor."

"I'm just bruised," she said weakly, but then she nearly tore his heart in two by wrapping her trembling arms around his neck and burying her face against his throat.

He took her up the stairs in order to avoid having to stop in the lobby. He didn't want to raise any questions about why he was carrying a woman, and after midnight the elevator cars coming up from the garage always stopped in the lobby for security reasons.

The stairs raised the inevitable possibility that he might encounter someone, but he listened carefully, planning to dart into a hallway if necessary. No such need arose at this hour. Dawn approached, still some hours away, but he could feel it in a prickling along his neck, a built-in timer.

If Yvonne needed a doctor, the situation could get very difficult.

Reaching his penthouse, he found the door still open as he had left it. Native caution made him sniff the air. In its scents he read the evening just past, but nothing new. Stepping inside, he kicked the door shut, pressed the lock button, and heard the dead bolts engage with a solid thunk.

Then he carried Yvonne to his bed, where he laid her down gently. She was still wide-eyed, still breathing too rapidly, and he smelled the fear that perfumed her enticing scent.

But nothing else. He studied her, looking for signs of internal injury, which would have shown as a heat bloom. When he found none, he released a breath he hadn't realized he'd been holding until that moment.

"Where do you hurt?" he asked her.

"My shoulder aches a little. But I'm fine, Creed. When he threw me, I slid more than I hit. I'm just glad I was wearing jeans and long sleeves."

But he saw no gladness in her green eyes. None at all. She looked haunted and hunted, and terrified. "What happened?" she asked thinly. "I couldn't see much."

Before he could answer, she saw his chest. A gasp escaped her and she sat bolt upright. "What happened to you?"

"A fly-by swipe," he answered, trying to sound humorous. "Don't worry, it's already healing. It'll be gone in an hour."

"Why did he hurt you? Why did he threaten to kill me? Creed, what's going on? Everyone talked around things at dinner and I just kept quiet because I didn't really know what to ask."

First he had something more important to deal with, and now that he knew she was all right, anger surged in him.

"How the hell did he get in here?"

Yvonne paled, maybe because there was no

mistaking the anger in his tone. "I, uh, opened the door."

"Did it never occur to you that might be a stupid thing to do?"

She reared up, her eyes sparking. "I'm not stupid. I knew what I was doing. I was getting out of here. I'm sick of being talked around, sick of not getting answers. I feel like a piece of baggage, and not one that's especially wanted!"

"Yvonne..."

"No, you've all made it clear. Especially you. I'm just a problem to be solved and I'm not even entitled to know what's going on. You keep dropping hints, but how the hell am I supposed to deal with all of this if you won't tell me what's going on? How was I to know that opening a door could get me kidnapped by a vampire when you won't even tell me?"

Creed's anger faded before the force of what she was saying. He couldn't deny it. Oh, he'd been all up front about telling her he was a vampire, but then he'd basically left her dangling in the wind with heavy hints and little information.

At last he sighed, dreading all the thorny places these questions would take him. Then he gathered her close and just held her, drinking in her warmth and scent like a drug. For once they calmed him, rather than arousing him. He felt oddly grateful that she didn't make even a small attempt to escape his embrace. She'd have been entitled to.

"After my change," he said slowly, "it felt as if the entire world had gone mad. It must have felt that way tonight to you, especially after Luc grabbed you. I am so, so sorry."

Her arms slipped hesitantly around him, and he reveled in the sensation. "It did seem crazy. I honestly wasn't sure what was happening until he stopped. My God, he was moving so fast it was like being on a crazy carousel. I couldn't even see!"

"I know."

"But why did he want to kill me?"

"He's not thinking clearly now." Nor was *he,* come to that, because right now all he wanted to do was bury his body inside hers, and sip her blood, just a little bit….

He drew away quickly, leaving her gasping.

"Sorry," he said, his voice tight. "I need blood to heal." He headed for the fridge, knowing it was just an excuse to tamp down his urges. He wasn't so hungry that he needed it, but he was hungry for *her* which made it essential.

"Then drink mine."

The words froze him in midstep. Several seconds, at least several, ticked by before he could bring himself to answer. "No. Don't be crazy."

"I'm not being crazy. I hate being dependent on you. I hate being a leech on your life. Even more, I hate knowing that having me around torments you. But I can't figure out what to do. I was going to leave tonight. I was heading out the door when Luc got me. Apparently I can't stop leaning on you. Giving you a little blood hardly seems like enough to pay you back."

"No. You don't owe me a thing. And for the love of heaven, don't you dare try to leave again. You're in danger!"

"I know that. And I owe you plenty. Creed, you just saved my life!"

"I don't want payback. I don't want it." He whirled to face her, aware that his eyes must be as black as pitch. "That's the last way I want your blood. You insult me!"

She gasped, and horror filled her face. "I didn't mean…"

"Yes, you did. I guess in your mind I don't even qualify as a friend. I'm just hired help, to be paid in some coin or other. And that's an insult to me and my motives."

He turned, grabbed a bag from the fridge and headed out into the living room, where he ignored the nicety of using a glass and simply tore into the bag of blood with his teeth, sucking it dry.

His chest, already healing, still hurt. But other things hurt worse. Now he knew where he fit on Yvonne's scale. In her eyes, his motives couldn't possibly be pure. The sharpest cut of all.

"Creed." Her voice came from behind him and he stiffened. "Creed, I didn't mean it that way."

He closed his eyes, squeezing the bag of blood in his fist until one of the last few drops oozed out. He smelled it, felt it run over his hand. "Isn't it past your bedtime?"

He heard a soft cry escape her. Listened as she whirled and went back into his bedroom. He wondered if she would lock him out, leaving him to the mercies of dawn. Part of him hoped she would.

But she didn't. She didn't close the door even a bit.

Maybe that meant something.

Or not.

Yes, it was past her bedtime, but sleep eluded Yvonne. If anything, the night's events had left her so far awake that she wondered if she'd ever sleep again.

First that shocking abduction by a vampire. Things happening so fast that she hadn't been sure *what* was happening until Luc stopped in the garage and threatened to snap her in two. Her heart slammed at the mere memory of the threat, for she had felt his unbreakable strength when she had tried to struggle, in the moments before the world began moving so fast that terror had frozen her, and again when they had stopped.

The fall through the stairwell had been a total blur, and she had barely grasped what had happened only when he paused to open the door into the parking garage.

Everything was a smear of wind, color and steel arms.

Then the encounter between Luc and Creed. Shocking in a different way. Even after she'd been thrown and lay stunned on the ground, she had felt power and menace unlike anything in her experience. Except possibly that thing in her condo.

And then she had managed to insult Creed so deeply that he didn't even want her apology or her explanation.

She rolled over, and buried her face in a pillow, trying to stave off tears. Too much was happening too fast, and she felt utterly overwhelmed. Just a few days ago—okay, little more than a week—she'd been living a very ordinary life. Then some presence had started haunting her home, she'd learned vampires were real, been told that a demon wanted her, then Luc had tried to abduct her and now Creed was mad at her…

A primal scream would have felt good right then, but instead she let hot tears flow. How could she have ever guessed that her very ordinary life was actually constructed on the tiny tip of a needle, and only a small push could change everything forever?

Only this had been more than a small push. More like getting hit by a freight train.

Too much. Way too much. If only she could burrow back through time and move into a different apartment.

But she couldn't be sure that would have changed a thing in the end, especially since Tommy might be at the root of all this. Except that she might never have come to know Creed.

And she wasn't sure that anything at all could make her wish that had never happened.

She thought her tears were silent, but apparently something had alerted Creed. All of a sudden he sat on the bed's edge and touched her shoulder lightly. "Are you hurting?"

At first she didn't even want to answer. But finally she squeezed out a few words. "Only my heart."

Silence. Absolute, profound silence. From what she could tell, he didn't even stir to draw a breath.

"Yvonne…"

When he didn't continue, she reluctantly rolled over. She couldn't let him continue to think that she had meant to insult him. "It's not you," she said, her voice breaking. "It's me. I hate being beholden. I hate it."

"You owe me nothing."

"I know. You never asked for a thing. But… it's how *I* feel. I feel like I'm taking so much. I'm a burden. I know it's hard for you to have me around. Terri told me tonight…" She trailed off, unable to continue.

"Ah," he said quietly. "Terri."

"She didn't do anything wrong. It's just that I didn't fully understand how hard it must be for you to have me around all the time. And that made me feel awful. Just awful! You didn't ask for this, but here you are stuck with a human who must be testing your self-control every single minute. I feel terrible about that. Horrible about the way I've had to impose on you."

His eyes, she saw, had lost their blackness and grown more golden. That beautiful gold that always struck her.

"Let me explain," he said quietly. "I chose to invite you here. No one made me offer my protection."

"Jude…"

"Jude asked me to take you home and check

your apartment. Beyond that, everything was my choice. I could, if I had wanted, let you go to a hotel. Or taken you back to Jude. There were other options. I was actually glad to be able to offer you some security. It's been a long time since I could do that for anyone."

She felt a flutter in the pit of her stomach. "But it's hard on you."

"Little worth doing is ever easy." The faintest of smiles curved his mouth. "I freely admit that my craving for you surpasses description. But telling myself no also builds my character, don't you think?"

A damp, tear-choked laugh escaped her. "Why is everything painful supposed to build our characters?"

He shrugged, looking more amused now. "Beats me. But nobody gets all the way through life the easy way. Nobody."

He lifted his head, as if sensing something. Then he hesitated. "We have time to go visit my friend Avi, if you feel brave enough to let me carry you there, it's faster than a car."

She realized she hadn't minded at all when Creed carried her. A whole different thing than when Luc had snatched her. In fact, she thought, tipping her head, it might be an interesting experience to repeat when she wasn't terrified.

"Sure," she said. "Do I need to close my eyes?"

"It won't do you much good to keep them open. I move faster than your brain can register visually. You'll have to cling to my back though, because I'm going over the rooftops."

"Wow. I hope I can see something."

He laughed. "Who knows? Maybe you will. You often astonish me."

He insisted she wrap up against the night chill while he called Avi Herschel. Yvonne was surprised that anyone was answering their phone this late at night, but before she could get around to asking about it, Creed scooped her up, settled her on his back and they were off.

Not out his door and down the stairwell, but over the edge of the terrace. That was the last thing she could truly see as the wind bit sharply at her face. Her surroundings passed in an amazing blur of shadow and colored light, so fast that she instinctively gasped for air and buried her face against Creed's back.

The next thing she knew, they had come to

a stop. When she lifted her head, she could see that they stood on a small balcony, mostly a fire escape landing, outside a window. Creed lowered her carefully to her feet.

"We're here," he said.

While he rapped on the window, she looked around, trying to figure out where she was. It was certainly a long way from the high-end condos where she and Creed lived.

The window slid open with a creak, and a surprisingly young, bearded face peeked out.

"Creed," a jovial voice said with evident pleasure. Then a pair of dark eyes settled on Yvonne. "Who is this?"

"My friend Yvonne. She can be trusted."

Avi sniffed the air in a way she was coming to know. Then he looked at the slashed front of Creed's shirt, where gashes still showed.

"And you. Are you bringing trouble?"

"Not to you, of that I'm sure."

"If you say so," Avi said after a moment. "Come in, come in."

Creed helped her over the window ledge then followed her inside. The dimly lit apartment was decorated with furnishings from a much older era and smelled a bit musty. Books were stacked everywhere, having overflowed the floor-to-ceiling bookcases. A few dim lamps were lit, and she wondered how anyone could see to read by them.

Then it struck her: Avi Herschel must be a vampire, too.

At once she wanted to find a seat. As if sensing it, Creed guided her to an armchair. When she sat, a cloud of dust seemed to rise.

"So," said Avi, eying her cautiously, "you trust her."

"Obviously, or I wouldn't have brought her. We don't have much time."

"No." Avi sighed and stroked his beard. "I'm sorry, dear lady, but I don't have any refreshment to offer you. I'm not used to…visitors of your kind."

"It's all right," Yvonne managed, feeling awfully uncertain about this development. "Thank you for thinking of it."

"I still have manners, even after all these centuries. Breaking bread, sharing tea, these are important things."

"Avi," Creed said with a touch of impatience, "on to business. We don't have time to be social."

Avi waved a hand then settled into a creaky wood chair in front of an ancient wood desk. "There is always time to be polite."

"Unless the sun is about to rise. Asmodai seems to have his eye on my friend here."

"Ah, that's not good!" Avi muttered something into his beard. Then his dark gaze settled on Yvonne. "So next time I will have some tea for you. A nice, strong Russian blend."

"Thank you." Yvonne wondered if she was slipping down some kind of rabbit hole. What was all this with tea?

"Avi," Creed said a touch impatiently. "Time. Sun. Asmodai."

"Right." Avi's attention swung to Creed again. "That one, he's always causing trouble with the ladies." He looked once more at Yvonne. "A lovely lady, too." Then he sighed. "My dear woman, you must understand the world is full of things, many which you have never seen, and many which, God willing, you will never see. Asmodai is an angel."

"An angel!"

Avi nodded. "I've been studying the subject for several thousand years and I'm not quite sure I understand."

Yvonne was stunned. Several thousand years? He couldn't possibly mean that! But of course, in this new world in which she existed, it seemed he could. She looked desperately at Creed.

"Avi," he said, "this is helping how?"

"You must understand the nature of the beast."

"So you say he's an angel. Well, what do we know about angels?"

"That they can be terrible beings indeed. What we know about this one is small but significant. He was not cast out of heaven. So it becomes a question of his purpose when he does ill."

Creed finally sat down. "That *is* a good question."

"His true purpose is shrouded, but it is evident he hasn't done all that much harm…except for his proclivity for human women."

"Indeed," Creed said drily. "Well, he's apparently arranging a circle in order to come through in physical form. We need to bind him when he tries. I understand the Tetragrammaton will do the job?"

"Well, you must ask yourself what you

hope to accomplish. Asmodai will avoid the Tetragrammaton." He returned his attention to Yvonne, apparently enjoying having a pupil. "The four letters that represent the unpronounceable name of God. They also stand for 'I am' which raises the question of whether they are a name at all."

"Avi…"

"Easy, my friend. The sun comes I know. But after all these millennia, I have no students, only colleagues. It is fun to explain." He sighed.

"So what do you mean, it depends on what we want to do with Asmodai?"

"Do you want to build a temple?"

"No."

"I thought not. When Solomon chained the Tetragrammaton around Asmodai's neck, he enslaved him. I don't think you want a slave."

"No, actually I don't. I just want him to get out of this world, or prevent him from coming into it physically."

"Well, I'm not absolutely certain you can do that."

Yvonne gasped. Creed looked ready to grind his teeth.

"You see," Avi continued, "Asmodai used to come and go at will. Now he seems to have lost his ability to come and go as he chooses. We suspect he may have been punished."

"But you don't know."

"How can we? Does heaven talk to us? Do I have a phone line there? Has any angel come to me to say Asmodai has been cast out? But I suspect he has."

"Which would explain his need for a human pentagram to return."

"So it seems."

"Any idea how we should handle this?"

Avi leaned back, stroking his beard thoughtfully. "I must think about this."

"The sun."

"I know. Go. I will think. Come back tonight, late. You don't want to enslave him, but you need to send him back." He turned and picked up a volume that looked several centuries old and blew the dust off it. "Look through this. I will do some thinking. Maybe between us we will solve the problem."

Creed pulled a drawstring bag out of one of his pockets. "Think hard, Avi," he said as he stuffed the ancient volume into it and strung it from his wrist.

Then he turned and swung Yvonne onto his back. This time she seemed more aware of the world's passage, or perhaps Creed moved more slowly. What little she could sense, from the flexing of powerful muscles in his back, to the world whizzing by, overwhelmed her, but with delight.

The next thing she knew, he was setting her gently down on his terrace. He opened the sliding door and let them both in.

"Dawn is getting closer. We have a little while yet before I have to lock us in. Do you want to freshen up and get ready for bed first?"

She hesitated. "I really want some answers."

"All right. I'll gather some food and coffee so you can be comfortable tomorrow. So where do you want to start with your questions?"

"Honestly, Creed, I don't know anymore." She started to reach out toward his gashed chest and slashed shirt, but snatched her hand back at once, realizing that might make it harder for him. "You *are* healing."

"It was minor. His nails raked me."

"That was some rake." When combined with

the steely strength she had felt in Luc's arms, she could easily imagine that a vampire's nails were more like talons. They were predators. Creed had said so. Of course they would have weapons in addition to their speed. "I was so scared," she admitted.

"I'm not surprised. My kind can be terrifying indeed, and Luc is on the edge."

"The edge of what?" She waited, watching him as he started gathering food and coffee for her. She wondered if time was really that short or if he was keeping himself busy while he thought of ways to answer difficult questions.

She trotted after him into the bedroom as he carried an armload of supplies for her along with the coffeemaker. She hoped he would just be honest with her because at this point, despite all the shocks she had endured, she felt half truths would only make things worse. "Creed, I need to know what I'm dealing with. There's no way now I'm going to get through this in ignorance."

"I suppose not." He set things down beside her laptop, then looked away from her, his gaze growing distant. "You heard us talk about Luc wanting to avenge the death of his mate, Natasha."

"Yes. And there was something about it. But I don't remember the word." She sat on the edge of the bed, waiting.

"Claiming. There's no exact parallel for it among your kind. When a vampire claims someone or something, in this case a mate, possession becomes obsession beyond anything you can likely imagine. Natasha was Luc's claimed mate. It's not a choice, Yvonne. It just happens. And when it does, there's nothing that can break it for the vampire except his or her own death, or in this case, vengeance."

Yvonne shook her head a little, unable to grasp exactly what he meant.

"Let me try this another way," Creed said. "Luc is not responsible for what he's doing. He can't help it. He claimed Natasha, and she was killed. For a vampire, this death induces a kind of insanity. The pain is intolerable from what I've seen and heard. So start from the point that Luc is insane. I'm just glad I was able to get through to him."

Yvonne shuddered, remembering the strength of those arms, the threat to snap her in two. She had no doubt Luc could have done it. “So how can you help him?”

“He needs to take vengeance. That’s the only way other than death to break the obsession, and honestly it doesn’t always work.” He paused. “Jude has claimed Terri, you know. He warned her that if he did, she’d never be able to leave him because he’d follow her to the ends of the earth. There’d be nowhere she could hide. The truth is, I think he’d die before he did that to her, but it’s always a possibility.”

“She loves him, though.”

“Definitely. She’s also a mortal. At some point he’s going to have to decide whether to change her to keep her, or face the insanity that will come with losing her.”

“But she wants to be changed.”

Creed nodded. “The question is whether Jude will ever think that’s the right thing to do.”

“Why would he hesitate? The way you two live, it doesn’t seem to be such an awful thing.”

“Ah, my sweet morsel,” he said with a sad smile, “you don’t know what it’s like to be a newborn vampire.”

“Not good?”

"Extremely painful. The hunger is overwhelming. The desire to feed is uncontrollable. Her instincts could well drive her to do things she would never forgive herself for, and then Jude would never forgive himself. Frankly, Yvonne, I can't imagine the horror of watching someone you love go through this change. Of knowing that however well they managed to get through it, you've condemned them to an eternity of wanting what they can never have."

Before she could ask another question, the doorbell rang. Creed stiffened, glancing at the bedside clock. "Stay here," he said.

Then moving so swiftly she never saw him go, he vanished.

Creed opened the door when he saw Chloe on his CCTV screen.

"I was on my way home," Chloe snapped as she stepped into Creed's apartment. "Then this guy waylaid me." She jerked her head, indicating Luc St. Just.

Creed tensed, ready to spring. "What the hell are you doing, Luc?"

"Good question," Chloe said. "I'm finally heading for my own bed, when all of a sudden

I get hijacked by a vampire. Cripes, Creed, I don't even have my car. How am I going to get home now?"

Luc stepped completely into Creed's line of sight. "I don't have long. I came to apologize."

Creed hesitated, feeling utter distrust. "I'm supposed to believe that?"

"I owe a lady an apology. I brought Chloe to get you to open the door." He glanced at Chloe who was glaring at him. "I guess I owe this lady an apology, too."

"You owe me more than that, you blood-sucking jerk! I don't care what kind of vampire madness you suffer from, you just don't grab people off the street, scare them half to death, take them on a roller coaster ride at high speed, and get off with an apology!"

Luc looked at her, his expression unreadable. "Would having me take a walk in the sunlight make you happy?"

"Nothing's going to make me happy right now," Chloe grumped. "Damn it, I need my sleep. Where's the coffeepot, Creed? Sheesh, you put the dang thing away?"

Creed never even glanced at Chloe as she marched toward his kitchenette. Not once did he take his attention from Luc. "The pot is in the bedroom, Chloe. Luc, give me one good reason I should let you in."

"How about that you're right? That working together will get us further than me mucking around on my own."

Creed studied him, saw that his eyes were golden, not black anymore. At this point, he didn't see he had much choice. From the moment he'd opened his door, the chance that he could close it before Luc entered had become slim.

"Just watch it," he said, and made way for the other vampire.

Luc slipped inside to the end of the living room farthest from the bedroom. Since Luc could undoubtedly smell exactly where Yvonne was, he supposed that was a good sign. He closed the door, the deadbolts slid into place, and he faced the other vampire.

Chloe emerged from the bedroom with the coffeemaker and banged around the kitchen making coffee, muttering about "damn vampires." Moments later, Creed sensed Yvonne in the bedroom doorway behind him.

But Luc didn't even glance at her. He seemed fixed on Creed.

"You're right," Luc said again.

"He's often right," Chloe commented sourly. "Mainly because he's brilliant, unlike a certain vampire I just unwillingly met."

"My apologies, madam."

"Spare me. Now I'm going to have to take the bus home. I hate the bus."

"What's going on?" Yvonne asked. Her voice was thin with fright. The smell of her fear saturated the air along with her other enticing scents. Creed saw Luc's nostrils flare in response. His own did as well, but he didn't dare take his gaze from Luc.

"I owe you an apology, too," Luc said to Creed. "I frightened your lady. I hope I didn't hurt her. But I know better than that."

"She's not…"

Luc shook his head. "Maybe you don't know it yet. But I feel it. So I am here to apologize. To her, to you, and now to your friend whom I so shamelessly used."

Chloe spoke as she spooned coffee into the basket. "At least he admits it was shameless."

"It was," Luc agreed. "I needed an entrée,

madam, and after what I did tonight, I was certain of only one way to get it."

Chloe turned from the coffeepot and placed her palms on the bar. "I don't like being used. I'm not your entrée to anything. And if you use me to hurt Creed or Yvonne, I'll find a way to stake your dead bones out in the daylight. Trust me, I will."

Creed was surprised to see the faintest of smiles curve Luc's mouth. Given the vampire's overall state of mind, that was a good sign.

"If I should behave so foolishly again, I will allow you to stake out my dead bones."

Chloe sniffed and turned back to the coffeepot. Creed noted that Yvonne had edged into the room, and was joining Chloe in the kitchen. She felt safer with *Chloe?* Another wound.

"That's all I came for," Luc said after a moment. "To apologize. *Mes excuses plus profondes.* My most profound apologies to you all. And to ask that I be allowed to cooperate in your effort."

Before Creed could reply, Chloe whirled around again. "The *person* you need to ask is Jude. He's the one who knows how to deal with this stuff. And I'm not sure he's going to trust you after what you did to me." She turned suddenly to Yvonne. "Did I get that right? Did that vampire do something to you, too?"

Yvonne nodded. "He tried to abduct me."

"Lovely!" Chloe threw up a hand. "And now we're supposed to trust him? Two kidnappings in one night?" She stuffed a hand into the pocket of her tight black leather skirt—Creed wondered how she could fit anything into a pocket on a garment so snug—and pulled out a cell phone. She flipped it open, pressed a button and waited all of two seconds.

"Boss. No, I don't want to hear what time it is. I already know. Leave Terri alone for a minute. We've got a problem named Luc St. Just. Oh, just a little matter of two abductions tonight, namely Yvonne and me. Yeah, we're okay. And now he's apologizing and wants to join us in the current mess. Uh-huh. I know. No, I don't know how I'm going to get home. I'm at Creed's right now, the damn sun is due up in a few minutes, and I doubt either one of these vampires could get me home in time for them to go to ground. In fact, I'm looking at one of them right now thinking he's cutting it pretty fine. What? Sheesh. Okay." She held her phone out to Creed. "He wants to talk to you. He said something about not having time for my babble."

Creed had to swallow a laugh. Jude could be so acidic when Chloe got on a rant. He took the phone, saying, "Hello."

"Well," Jude's voice said in his ear, "it sounds like you've had an exciting night. I can tell Chloe's okay, but what about Yvonne?"

"She's bruised and shaken, but otherwise fine. I wouldn't blame her if she asked me to stake St. Just out in the sun, though."

"Me, either," Jude replied. He was silent a moment, then asked, "What's your evaluation of Luc? Can we trust him?"

"What other option do we have?"

"Good point. We've either got him going rogue or we bring him in."

"That would be my estimation. I also had a rather cryptic conversation with my friend Avi."

"That doesn't sound good." Jude sighed. "It's too late to talk. Tell St. Just to be at my office tonight at ten. You and Yvonne come, as well. We're going to sort things out."

Creed snapped the phone shut and passed it back to Chloe, then looked at Luc.

"Well?" Luc asked.

Creed, who felt the sun's approach as a maddening prickle on the back of his neck, a prickle that strengthened with every passing second, wondered if Luc was suicidal. He was dallying too long.

"Jude's office tonight at ten. We'll all discuss you and your involvement. Which right now I would much rather do without."

Luc's gaze flickered, the first sign he had shown of true regret. "Until tonight," he said, then vanished from the apartment.

Chloe leaned forward on her elbows while coffee brewed behind her. "Can I say that that was not the most enjoyable experience of my life?"

"I know," Yvonne remarked. "Trust me, I know. I was terrified."

"At least I figured out what was happening. You must have been totally shocked. I just got furious."

"Understandable," Creed said as he went to close and lock the door. "I apologize to both of you. Sometimes the behavior of my kind leaves much to be desired."

Chloe sighed. "I understand the claiming thing. Really I do. Jude was willing to be turned into a torch rather than let a demon harm Terri. But this kidnapping thing… I'd like to slap Luc upside the head."

A little giggle escaped Yvonne, surprising Creed. "I think you'd break your hand, Chloe."

"Yeah. These vampires are so damn hardheaded." She blew a noisy sigh and turned back to the coffeepot. "Man, I need that caffeine. The bus ride to my house will take almost two hours. Stupid vampire."

"You can stay here," Creed offered. "The couch is comfortable."

"I wanted my own bed for a change. Every time we get involved in one of these cases, I forget what it's like to sleep in my own bed, use my own shower…" She trailed off and suddenly grinned. "Whine, whine. I know. I guess I'm an adrenaline junkie, and I sure got a shot of it tonight. You want me to watch Yvonne while you sleep? Or are you handling this some other way?"

Creed looked at Yvonne. "I've been keeping her close. But I suppose it's up to her."

Yvonne surprised him by her lack of hesitation. "No offense, Chloe, but I feel safer locked in with Creed."

Chloe shrugged. "Frankly, I would, too. And time's wasting. So you'd better get in there."

Indeed, Creed thought as the tingling on his neck reached the discomfort level.

"I need to get some things in the bedroom for Yvonne. Like the coffeepot..." He stared pointedly at the pot Chloe had just made.

"Ah hell," Chloe said.

"No, it's all right, I'll be fine," Yvonne protested.

"No," said Chloe and Creed at the same instant, "you won't be." They looked at each other, and a laugh escaped Chloe.

"Go ahead, Creed," she said. "Take it into the bedroom for her. I'll sail out of here anyway after a quick nap."

Not needing to conceal his speed, it didn't take Creed long to move things into the bedroom to ensure Yvonne's comfort if she woke before nightfall.

Mere seconds later, he stood in the doorway to his bedroom. “Ready, Yvonne?”

“Ready is a word that doesn’t seem to apply around you,” she remarked.

“How so?”

“You do everything so fast that I barely get time to blink before everything has changed.”

In spite of himself, he grinned as she eased past him into the bedroom.

“See you tonight,” Chloe called after them.

Inside the bedroom, Creed closed and locked the door. “I guess I’ll have to clean up later,” he said. “Any minute now…”

“I know.” Yvonne stretched out on the bed. “I’ll wash up after you go to sleep.”

The pull of death was growing stronger. He felt it coming like a panther determined to devour him. He started to lower himself to the floor but Yvonne stopped him.

“Creed?”

“Yes?”

“If all I can give you is some warmth, please let me. If it won’t be too uncomfortable.”

Oddly, that seemed like the most comfortable thing in the world. As the sleep of death approached, other instincts grew weaker because he couldn't act on them. Surely it was safe in the twilight between waking and death?

So he lay beside her on the bed, on his back. And when she curled close, resting her arm over his waist, her warmth breath caressing his neck, he felt a warmth that far exceeded any he had ever known as a mortal. It was a gift the beauty of which she could not begin to imagine.

"Thank you," he managed to whisper. Then, feeling safe in the twilight place, he fought back sleep and turned toward her wrapping her in his arms. He should have been surprised but somehow he wasn't when she moved even closer, pressing her length to him.

He was past feeling the sexual, only aware of her wonderful warmth. "If you grow uncomfortable, just move," he said.

Then death claimed him, a dark emptiness where not even dreams could find him.

Chapter 8

Much to her amazement, Yvonne slept the entire day away. Apparently stress and fatigue had caught up with her, but when she awoke she was curled tightly around Creed, who felt cooler now than when she had fallen asleep. Wrapped in her favorite blue sweat suit, she felt warm enough, and found it easy to wind herself around him, although she wondered if he could feel the heat of her body in his….

In his what? Was he really dead? She couldn't tell if he was breathing, and when she laid her head on his chest, she heard no heartbeat. Yet he said he could be wakened if necessary, so he couldn't really be dead.

The ravages Luc had wrought on his chest were gone as if they had never been, the shredded, slightly bloody shirt the only evidence.

She studied him in awe, and something warm curled up like a kitten in her heart. He had trusted her completely. Trusted her not to harm him when he was as helpless as he could be. Trusted her not to fling the door open and let the light in. Trusted her not to take advantage of his helplessness.

That was trust indeed.

Sighing, she laid her head on his shoulder again and waited for some sign of life. It wouldn't be long now, she was certain.

She wanted to share the moment with him, to truly see what it was like. He called it resurrecting. Was that really what it was?

Ordinarily she would have been annoyed with herself for missing an entire day's writing, but not today. She had needed the sleep. Even more she had seemed to need these moments of intimacy, to realize what he had offered her.

To face the fact that he had given her utter trust and that she seemed to be unable to give him the same. Her cheeks heated when she remembered his response to her offer to give him her blood. Now that she was calmer, she could easily understand why he had been so offended.

He was not her mother. Not by the least word or sign had he indicated that she was an unwanted burden. Maybe she could learn from him.

Maybe she could learn for the first time that friendship need not be a debt that must somehow be repaid. That it was possible to act out of sheer kindness without expecting something back.

She wrote such characters in her novels all the time. But they were, to her way of thinking, a mythical ideal, as mythical as the creatures she created out of whole cloth. Heroes of fantasy, never of reality.

Just then an ugly thought wound its way into her head and made her nearly gasp with pain. So he said she owed him nothing? But what if that was because he was being paid to watch her? Before she could even begin to deal with how that idea made her feel, he awoke.

She felt Creed jerk and heard him draw a sharp breath. She lifted her head at once and found his face locked into a grimace, his eyes wide open. Then he drew another breath, and his expression relaxed.

Slowly his black-as-night eyes tracked to her. "Have you been here all day?"

"Mostly. I slept. Does it hurt when you wake up?"

"As if every cell in my body is filled with fire. It passes quickly." He smiled almost gently. "Your warmth. Thank you. It feels especially good right now."

So she curled in closer, because it seemed like the least she could do. But the ugly question wouldn't rest. "Is Jude paying you to help me?"

"No. I don't need money." He fell silent for a moment, then to her amazement she felt him stroke her hair gently. "Are you still questioning my motives?" At least now he didn't sound angry about it.

"No. Not exactly. I just…I have a hang-up."

"About what?"

"I don't ever again want to be a burden."

"Who taught you that?"

She turned her head to conceal her face from him, and even then the words didn't seem to want to come. It was one of those things she could think about, when she let herself, but never had spoken about. In some essential way she felt shamed.

"Yvonne? Did no one ever teach you that some burdens can be borne with joy?"

She caught her breath. His words seemed to plummet straight to her heart. "No."

He fell silent for a minute, still stroking her hair lightly. "When I was a father, my children could sometimes be burdensome. Things they needed or wanted. It was my greatest joy to be able to provide for them. I never begrudged it. Well, all right, almost never. There were a few silly things they wanted that irritated me. But mostly I felt happy about meeting their needs. And I missed it when I could no longer do it except from a distance."

Yvonne's heart squeezed painfully, for herself, for him. "How did you help from a distance?"

"I was always able to see that they had enough to eat, adequate shelter even in hard times. Medical care when they couldn't afford it. Sometimes I think I may have helped too much because I felt so awful at having to abandon them in every other way. But when I could do something to make their lives easier or better, it was my privilege to do so. I still watch over my great-grandchildren, although by and large they need almost nothing that I'm able to give."

He stopped stroking her hair, caught her beneath the chin with one fingertip, and turned her face up. "Who made you feel like such a burden?"

She answered obliquely. "I wish I'd had a parent like you."

His face stilled. His dark gaze grew distant. "I see," he said finally, and she believed he did. Then he looked at her again and gave her a crooked smile. "I'd much rather be your lover than your parent, if you don't mind."

Her world tilted in an instant, and her insides turned warm and syrupy. Time seemed to slow down as she hovered in exquisite and painful anticipation and hope. All the things she had been worrying about and trying to work out vanished in a yearning so intense she felt like a drawn bow.

His arms snaked around her gently, though she could feel the strength in them, and he turned until they met face-to-face, body-to-body. Shocks erupted from every point of contact. She drew a deep, quick breath as she melted into him and gazed into his eyes.

They were golden, gloriously golden.

"You are so beautiful," he said, sliding his fingers into her hair to cup the back of her head. "You have no idea. And you're not just beautiful. Your scent is intoxicating."

She offered no more than an incoherent murmur in response.

"Tell me if I frighten you," he said.

Her heart nearly stopped. Frighten her how? She didn't care because she was certain that all she wanted right now was to find out what it was like to make love to a vampire. All his warnings couldn't quell her desire for him.

And he seemed about to…about to…

Slowly, very slowly as if to give her every chance to object, he moved his face closer and finally their lips touched. Lightly at first, then more hungrily as she arched into him, wanting, needing, to be closer.

His kiss was deep, passionate, stealing her breath and her mind along with it. She responded in kind, dimly aware she reached up to clasp the back of his head so he would not pull away.

She was going somewhere she had never gone before, of that she was certain. No kiss had ever stirred her like this, never had a simple kiss made her feel a prisoner to need.

When he at last tore his mouth from hers, she gasped desperately for air, but just as desperately tried to bring him back.

"Easy," he whispered. "Easy."

Easy? She didn't want easy. For the first time in her life she wanted to be conquered into total submission and carried away like a captive on the feelings he evoked.

He must have sensed her need, or smelled it, because he came back for another kiss, and another, lifting her higher into the universe of passion. But each time she tried to touch him, to pull at his clothing, to act on some of her feelings, he hushed her gently, soothed her to a lower plane of need.

Then she stiffened. Unmistakably she felt his teeth. A gentle nip just below her collarbone, not enough to break the skin she was sure. But that nip was the most electrifying thing he had yet done, and she heard herself saying, "Please, Creed. Oh, please!"

"Don't move," he said huskily. "Whatever you do, don't move."

She gave the barest nod of comprehension, stiffening herself to hold still. She felt the lap of his tongue, cool and soothing. Moments later her heart skipped into a higher rhythm, loud in her own ears. Or was that his heart? She couldn't tell… There seemed to be two heartbeats.

Orgasmic pleasure flooded her entire body, something she wouldn't have dreamed possible. Her brain fogged with yearning for more, and then she grew overwhelmed by a sense that she and Creed were one. His heart and hers, two hearts beating independently, began to beat in precisely matching rhythms. She lost all sense of where she ended and he began, and gave herself up to it.

His hands stroked her, kneading her breast to an aching peak. But more than what she felt in her own body, she was certain she was feeling it from his perspective, too. She was kneaded and stroked, and kneading and stroking.

And when his hand slipped down to touch

her between her legs, through layers of cloth, she felt not only her response, but his, a dual hit of desire, aching, yearning, throbbing, so magnified that it left her senseless of everything but sensation.

She didn't know how it was possible nor did she have the ability to wonder. Instead she felt racked, imprisoned in a cycle of need: him, her, the two of them, rising as one ever higher on pain and pleasure until she thought she would literally shatter.

Perfect. Perfect in every single instant. A rising tide of desire, hunger, need, lifted her up. Hers or his she couldn't tell. It was more than enough to be lifted, to be swept away toward a pinnacle she could barely imagine.

Each time their hearts throbbed, her body throbbed, too. Each breath she took was answered by a deep, quiet groan from him.

Then came exultation. She was feeding him in the way he most needed. At that moment she'd have gladly given him every drop of her blood, and died in a state of bliss.

All of a sudden, the connection vanished and she tumbled back to reality to feel him gently licking her skin where she had earlier felt his nip.

"I'm sorry," he said, lifting his head. "I shouldn't have done that. But I didn't take very much."

She didn't know what upset her more: having the incredible experience end this way or hearing him apologize for showing her a transcendent experience.

Feeling weak, wanting more, all she could do was press a finger to his lips. "No," she whispered. "Don't apologize. I wouldn't have missed that for anything."

His expression grew grim. "I was afraid of that."

Her voice grew stronger. "It's better to have some experiences only once than to miss them entirely."

His gaze leaped to hers, his yellow eyes intense. "Easy to say, hard to know. Never forget I'm a predator. I just crossed a line I shouldn't have. And now it'll be even harder not to cross it again."

She gasped, and in an instant he slid away. The next she saw of him, he stood in the bathroom doorway.

"I need to clean up, and need to think of other things than all the ways I want you. All the ways I'd like to love you." He paused, then added, "You really mustn't tempt me, Yvonne. All those things Luc did? I'm capable of them, too, and worse. Never forget, in my essential nature I'm a hunter, and I'm everything that goes along with that."

He left her breathless. Speechless. He closed the door quietly and she rolled back on the bed to stare at the ceiling. No one, absolutely no one, had ever made her feel like this before, as if she couldn't breathe, as if her body had turned to warm molasses. The fear he'd tried to make her feel couldn't even penetrate the heat and longing he'd aroused. And never, not even in the earliest, giddiest days with Tommy had she ever felt such a strong connection.

She was tempted to do something she had never done before: walk into that bathroom and make herself available. Instigate. Be bold.

But then she remembered his description of claiming. His self-proclamation that he was a predator. It was enough to nearly freeze her.

Not for herself, but for him. Did she want to risk causing him that kind of pain? Especially when she hardly knew him and couldn't begin to guarantee that she'd want to stay with him?

Questions swirled in her head as she continued to stare at the ceiling.

What was she getting into here? How far did she want to go? Even the threat of Asmodai seemed distant and inconsequential in comparison.

Not good, she thought, pushing herself off the bed. Somehow she had to get her priorities straight. First a demon who terrified her, one she hardly believed in though she had *felt* his presence. Then, and only then, other stuff.

Because then and only then could she be sure she was thinking straight, not just feeling.

And she knew all too well where these sorts of feelings had gotten her once before.

Beyond the windows, the last glow of the setting sun rimmed the world with gold, and clouds overhead gleamed striking colors of red.

Yvonne looked down at her coffee mug, trying to remembering the wanting, the hunger, she had felt only a short time ago. Her limited experience had taught her sex was nice, but not something worth craving. Now she craved Creed.

But with him, it was so much more complex than a powerful craving. There was danger involved, danger he kept trying to warn her about, and yet the danger only seemed to whet her appetite.

Suddenly she laughed. Talk about a new insight into herself!

"What's so funny?"

She turned and saw Creed emerging from the bedroom with a bag of blood in his hand.

"Oh, something I just realized about myself. I thought you didn't need to eat every day?"

"We're going to Jude's office. That means passing through the vampire deli of mortals going about their business on the streets, and spending time with a few humans who, I admit, tend to smell like a well-laid banquet table."

"Do I smell like that to you?"

"That and more. Much more. But it's best to be sated when I have to wander among mortals. I don't see the point in making temptation any harder to resist."

She touched her breast just below the collarbone, feeling again the tiny scabs. "You drank from me."

"Yes. Are you angry?"

"I seem to remember sort of asking you to."

"I didn't take much." He went into the kitchen and took out a glass to empty his meal into. "Far less than I could have taken without harming you."

"Why?"

He paused in the process of pouring blood into his glass. "Why?"

"Yes, why. If you can stop yourself, why didn't you take more?"

His brows knit. He finished pouring out the blood, then tossed the bag in the sink before coming to join her in the living area. The careful space was between them again, she noted, and felt a pang.

He spoke finally. "What did you think of the experience?"

"It was incredible." Her voice expressed her amazement. "I was… It was…"

He shook his head and smiled faintly. "You don't have to tell me. I was experiencing it with you. All of it."

"I felt… I felt like we were one."

"For a little while. My heart beats as yours beats. My body responds as yours does."

"How is that possible?"

"I don't know. It's the way it is. Everything in me seems to synchronize with you. Not just your heartbeat, but your feelings, as well. The danger is that you also synchronize with me."

"Wow." Astonished, even shocked, by the idea, she made her way to a chair and sat hunched with both her hands around her coffee cup. "Wow," she said again.

"That's part of what makes it so addicting. For both of us. The thing is, I stopped soon enough."

"Soon enough for what?"

"Soon enough that you didn't get addicted. Oh, you'll want to repeat the experience, I'm sure. Which is why I shouldn't have done it. But ask yourself if you want to experience it again enough to ask another vampire. Luc for example."

"Lord no!"

"Then you're still safe."

"You mean I might get to the point where I'd want just any vampire?" The thought appalled her.

"That's what I've been trying to tell you. It can happen. Well, I won't do that to you. I won't take you to the point where you'll spend the rest of your life hunting for another vampire. Any vampire." He sighed, then sipped his blood. "Damn, I don't know what got into me. I know you nearly craze me, I know I want you, but to give in and even give you a taste for me like that…" He shook his head in disgust.

"Don't beat yourself up."

He set his glass aside and came to kneel before her. He caught her face between his cool hands and made her look at him.

"Yvonne, we're playing with some serious fire here. I just found out that when it comes to you I can't always hold myself in check. That's dangerous for both of us."

She read his worry in his face and reached out to lay her palm against his cheek. At once his eyes closed, and a sigh escaped him, as if that simple touch were the most wonderful thing in the world.

And maybe it was. He could only feel warmth if it was human. He wanted her, he'd said as much many times. He'd warned her it was dangerous, he tried to keep a distance.

She remembered what Terri had told her and finally faced up to the fact that she was playing with fire all right.

"Should I leave?"

His eyes snapped open. "You wouldn't get very far. I'd follow. Don't even think of it. You're in worse danger than just me."

"Odd, I don't feel in danger from you at all. But I feel as if you're in danger from me."

A groan escaped him, and then before she could blink he was standing across the room. "I'm not in any danger I can't deal with," he said flatly. "Let's get that clear right now. You might drive me to the brink of madness, but I'll survive. What you absolutely, positively must not do is leave. It could cost you far more than I ever could."

"What's that?"

"Everything." He shook his head. "There are other realms than this one, other worlds and realities. Trust me, you wouldn't want to exist in whatever pit Asmodai is trying to climb out of. You wouldn't want to exist in *his* world. And you wouldn't enjoy your life here if he emerges and makes you his plaything."

"Is that what he's after? A sex slave?"

"I don't know, Yvonne. I just know he likes human women. He always has. What I'd like to know is if you've been offered to him in exchange for something else, because as beautiful as you are, there are other equally beautiful women."

Yvonne felt horror tingling along her nerves. "You *do* think Tommy is involved somehow. You think he offered me to that…that thing?"

He came closer and perched on the arm of a nearby chair, crossing his arms loosely. "What I know is that people who want things from demons must satisfy a demon's demands. Asmodai wants things, and he sets the price. His price is probably emergence into this world, and you. And perhaps some other things."

"But what could he give whoever summons him?"

"He might promise to perform some tasks. Might even promise great wealth and power. Sometimes demons even promise immortality, but they really can't keep that promise. Not for long."

"But you are immortal."

He shook his head. "No. I have a very long life. As you could see with Avi, it will be measured in thousands of years. But immortal life? No. Eventually we all die. There seems to be a natural order that cannot be defeated. To a gnat, you must look immortal."

She nodded slowly. "I suppose so."

"Now tell me about Tommy. What does he want?"

"That's easy. He wants to be a famous singer and musician. And he doesn't want to be a flash-in-the-pan, either."

"So, he would ask for fame and fortune as a rock star?"

"Probably. It's the only thing I ever saw him passionate about."

He smiled faintly. "But you don't think he'll make it on his own?"

"I don't like his music. He plays in small clubs, he's thirty and he's never had a nibble from a recording company even though he keeps sending demos."

"Well, that sounds like something Asmodai could promise. A lifetime of success, adoration and groupies."

Yvonne nodded glumly. "He'd go for that, all right."

"We'll ask Garner to look into it tonight."

"Garner?" She felt surprised.

"Oh, trust me, Garner is better at what he does than Jude lets on. The comments are merely a way to keep the rambunctious pup in line. But if he weren't good, Jude wouldn't put up with him."

"Is Jude very impatient?"

"He can be. But I actually think he enjoys being sardonic and sarcastic. Must be something left over from the world he grew up in."

"And that was?"

"A scion of nobility in an era where good form was everything, and good form apparently involved heavy doses of boredom, cynicism and world-weariness. Jude's rather a passionate sort, but he hides it behind a cultivated sarcasm."

"Well, I like him, but I like you better."

"What? This old professor? I'm boring."

"Not to me."

"Well, then, I'll become boring for a while. I need to look at that book Avi gave me."

She watched him pick it up from the table where he'd left it, blowing more dust off of it. Then he settled in an armchair and opened it. Curious, she rose and walked over to see pages yellowed and crinkled with age, and covered with characters she didn't recognize.

"Is that Hebrew?" she asked.

"Actually, no. Avi assures me it's angelic script."

"Really? And you can read it?"

"I've had a lot of time to learn to read things like this. Give anyone a century pretty much alone, and either he learns new things or he becomes the 'idle hands' of the aphorism. My kind in particular."

For the first time she wondered just how many esoteric things filled his head, and wished she could ask. But he was busy now, so she went to get herself another cup of coffee and a couple of cookies. Back on the sofa, she waited patiently, letting her thoughts roam freely, distracted only when she noticed how fast he seemed to be turning those pages. Evidently his speed wasn't limited to traveling.

She was just beginning to drift away into a dreamy sort of state as she recalled what it had been like to be drunk from by Creed. As a writer, she wanted to put it into words, to capture it in a way she could record, but it kept slipping out of her grasp, something so incredible her brain couldn't quite latch onto it.

Tommy had been her only lover, and in the early days she had been sure nothing could have been better. Well, there now was something in her experience so far beyond it that she couldn't capture it. Shattering, in a way, leaving her certain that she would never be the same.

That was what Creed feared for her. Exactly what he was trying to protect her from. Except she didn't want to be protected. Not from that, not from him.

Not that it made any difference what she wanted; Creed had made it obvious what he did not want.

She sighed silently, then stiffened. Sitting up straighter she waited, then was sure.

That thing was watching her again. The back of her neck prickled with awareness, but when she looked at Creed he was still reading, near the end of the book.

She hesitated, wondering if she imagined the sensation. What could possibly be watching her?

But the feeling grew, beginning to creep down her spine like a chill.

"Creed?" Her voice was thin.

"Yes?" He didn't look up.

"It's here. I feel it."

At once he snapped the book shut and an instant later he stood over her. He sniffed the air around her several times.

"Where's your coat?"

She waved vaguely toward the spare bedroom where she had dumped it last night. He vanished in a flash, then reappeared like magic with her coat. "Put it on. We're getting out of here now."

"I'm not imagining it?"

"I'd recognize that stench anywhere. I never forget a smell."

With trembling hands, she pulled her coat on while rising to her feet. "How did it find me?" she whispered.

"It probably always knew where you were. It was just biding its time."

Horror slammed her. Always? God, how was she ever going to escape this?

Creed brushed her fumbling hands away and

fastened her coat for her. Then he scooped her up, settling her on his back.

"Where are we going?" she asked.

"To Jude. He's got enough wards on his office to hold off the entire army of hell. At the very least, he has keys to a number of churches. We may need one."

That sent another shiver racing through her, but all of a sudden she was racing through the chilly night, too fast to see much, aware of little more than the stinging cold, the bunching of Creed's muscles, the sensation of flying.

She tightened her legs around his waist and hung on for dear life.

Chapter 9

The next thing she knew, they were at the bottom of the steps that led from the street to Jude's office. Creed didn't even set her down, but ran a key card through a scanner then punched in a code. And instant later she heard bolts slam open. Only when they were inside, with the door closed, did Creed lower her back to her feet.

"That was some trip," she murmured, pressing her hands to her chilled cheeks.

"If we're going to make a habit of this," Creed remarked almost humorously, "I need to get you something to keep your face warm." He held out his hand and she took it gratefully.

Together they walked down the darkened hallway to the open door of Jude's office. Warm light spilled forth.

Inside they found Chloe at her desk. She arched both darkened eyebrows at them. "You're early."

"Asmodai came to my condo a short while ago," Creed replied. He guided Yvonne to the sofa, where he encouraged her to sit. "She needs a warm drink, Chloe. I think I nearly froze her."

"Travel by vampire does have a few disadvantages." Chloe pressed an intercom button. "Jude? You need to emerge from the depths. We've got trouble."

Then she rose and walked over to the kitchenette where she poured a steaming mug of coffee and brought it to Yvonne. "You going to be okay, sweetie?"

"I'm fine, just cold."

"Yeah, it occurs to me that clothes suitable for skiing might be good for traveling with a vampire. I figured that out last night, thanks to Luc."

Yvonne managed a weak giggle. "I like it with Creed, actually. But it is cold."

"Wind chill of minus ninety, I'm sure. It's a wonder they don't make sonic booms."

"We don't move *that* fast," Creed said drily. "Just nearly."

The door to Jude's inner office opened and he joined them, dressed in his familiar black silk shirt and black slacks. "What's up?"

"Asmodai," Creed answered. "He was sniffing around Yvonne in my apartment."

Jude frowned. "Not good."

"That was my feeling. So, will she be safe here or do I need to take her to a church?"

"I guess we'll find out. Chloe, where's that bottle of holy oil?"

"Do I need to remember everything for everyone?" But she crossed the room to a cabinet and brought it out. "Since I'm Wiccan, I think it would be best if you applied it."

"You mean since you're short and I can reach over the doors."

Chloe sniffed.

"I would suggest," Jude said to her, "that you add a few wards of your own."

At that Chloe's entire demeanor changed. "You think we need that much?"

"I don't know and I'd rather not find out."

"Good point." Seeming much more subdued, Chloe began hunting through the drawers of her desk.

Creed settled beside Yvonne and once again took her hand. She appreciated the gesture, the touch, the sense of safety it gave her. A short time later, Chloe was setting white candles around the room and lighting them, while Jude marked each doorway, wall and the one window with the holy oil.

"There," he said. "That should do it." Then he turned to Creed and Yvonne, bottle of oil still in his hand. "You realize that now he knows you're not alone, that *we're* involved."

Chloe muttered, "I knew there had to be a downside to this job. Other than being abducted by a vampire."

"I know," Creed said. "But I have nothing in my apartment to create a ward."

"Wouldn't matter since obviously he'd already penetrated the place. He's not here yet, though."

Jude handed the bottle of oil back to Chloe

who returned it to the cabinet. Then he perched on the chair beside Chloe's desk. "Okay, it's out of the bag now. You came here, as good as advertising I'm involved. That means Asmodai knows Yvonne isn't alone in this, and that you aren't the only one he has to worry about."

"How much do you think that will complicate matters?"

Jude shrugged. "Maybe some, but I'm not sure a whole lot. He still needs to get into this world to do his damage. Did you find out anything from your friend?"

"He gave me a book to read. Once I process what I read this evening, I may have some clues. It was a book about angels, written in angelic script, so I'm assuming it might have been written by an angel. Apparently they have trouble with each other from time to time. How much we can use of *their* methods for dealing with troublemakers I still haven't figured out. And Avi said he was going to do some additional research, too."

"That's good. No Tetragrammaton?"

"He asked me if I wanted to build a temple."

Jude looked astonished, then laughed. "I guess he takes the indirect route."

"Often enough. Basically he asked if we wanted to enslave Asmodai or banish him. Apparently the necklace with the Tetragrammaton would enslave him."

"No, we don't want that. I have no use for him."

"Nor I," said Yvonne. "I just want him to leave me alone. Leave all of us alone."

"It occurs to me," said Creed thoughtfully, "that if we were to enslave him we could just order him back to wherever he comes from."

For an instant no one moved or made a sound. Then Jude laughed and slapped his own thigh. "I like that. It has a certain elegance to it."

"But we can't be sure it would work or for how long." Creed settled back on the sofa. "I need a little time to absorb what I've read today, and to find out what Avi has discovered. We can't let this happen too fast."

"As if we're in control." The laughter disappeared from Jude's face. "Garner is out looking for the rest of the circle, but he still hasn't found them all."

"They may not have been possessed yet. And that reminds me. Has Garner found Yvonne's ex-boyfriend? I think he needs to insinuate himself with the guy. It seems he has the perfect mixture of desire and inadequacy to be easy prey for the likes of Asmodai."

"Which is?"

Yvonne spoke. "He wants desperately to be a rock star and he's about as musical as a tin pan."

This time it was Creed who laughed, but Jude nodded. "That would do it. Big dreams and no way to fulfill them. People have fallen sway to demons for a lot less. And Garner hasn't run across him yet. He doesn't seem to be at home often."

Jude pulled a phone from his pocket and punched a button. "Garner. Where are you? Yeah. No, I need you to do something else for me. Hold one a sec." He looked at Yvonne. "What's the name of your boyfriend's band?"

"Tommy and the Mechanics."

"Lovely," Creed murmured, eliciting a giggle from Yvonne.

"Garner," Jude said. "Have you heard of a band called Tommy and the Mechanics? Of course not. I'm assured they're abysmal. Find out where they are. Present yourself as a recording executive or talent scout. I think the lead singer, Tommy…" He arched a brow at Yvonne. "*He* is the lead singer?"

"Yes."

"Tommy Sincks, the guy I asked you to look for," Jude continued, "may be in this up to his neck. I need to know. Why, yesterday, of course. If you need anything to add to your powers of persuasion, let me know. In the meantime, get some money from an ATM and flash a wad appropriately." He fell silent a few moments, listening, then sighed. "Right now I don't want him to know *I'm* involved. Asmodai has been hanging around Yvonne again."

"Maybe I should go," Creed suggested. "Yvonne is safe with you."

Jude shook his head, holding up a hand. "Yes. I really don't care. Just do it." He snapped his phone closed.

"Jude," Creed began again, but Jude cut him off.

"Right now, Asmodai knows about you. He knows you came here. The one thing we can't be certain he knows about is Garner's involvement. So it makes more sense to send Garner after this Tommy cretin right now. If that doesn't work, I'll consider letting you play the knight errant, all right?"

Yvonne glanced at Creed, wondering how he felt about that, but his face was unreadable. He was still holding her hand and she turned hers so she could squeeze it.

He looked down at her, and his face softened a bit.

"I know how you feel," Jude remarked. "Trust me. Right now you want to tear Asmodai limb from limb. But right now we need to be reasonably cautious so we don't precipitate anything we're not ready to deal with. I need your brain power more than your acting abilities tonight."

"And," Creed finally agreed, "we still have to find a way to knit Luc St. Just into this."

"Ah, yes. St. Just. It just keeps getting lovelier, doesn't it?"

Chloe spoke. "Have you eaten today, Yvonne?"

"Not really." She hadn't even thought about it except for a couple of cookies.

Chloe snorted. "These vampires need some lessons in the care and feeding of humans." Jumping up from her desk, she grabbed her jacket and purse. "I'm going out to pick up something. Do you have a preference?"

"Anything is fine. Really. I'm sorry I don't have any money with me."

"Jude's paying," Chloe said saucily.

"Of course I am," Jude drawled.

"No, I will," Creed said, standing and pulling out a wallet. "At least let me do some damn little thing that doesn't leave me feeling utterly useless."

He passed some bills to Chloe and she pranced out the door with a toss of her head.

Jude looked at Creed. "Useless? Hardly."

"Certainly not," Yvonne said quickly. "You saved me from St. Just last night. And you're doing some important research. You've been protecting me for days."

"Well, I don't feel as if I've succeeded all that well."

"I'm still here and in one piece, aren't I?"

He frowned. Jude stood. "I'll let you two hash this out. Meanwhile, I have one word of advice for you, Creed."

Creed's frown deepened.

"Going off half-cocked out of impatience would be the worst thing any of us can do right now. And you really didn't need me to tell you that, did you?"

Jude disappeared into his office, closing the door behind him.

Creed sighed and looked down at Yvonne. "He's right, of course. None of us can afford to be rash. It isn't as if this is just another one of the common demons Jude has dealt with a hundred or a thousand times before. This is uncharted territory."

Yvonne reached out, seized his hand and tugged him down beside her on the couch. "I don't want you to be rash, and I don't want you to feel pressured to do something. I'd hate it if something happened to you."

He gave a bark of laughter. "Nothing's going to happen to *me*. I'm not worried about myself."

"You've never dealt with something like this before. How can you possibly be sure nothing's going to happen to you, especially when it apparently killed Natasha?"

"I suspect Natasha may not have been entirely innocent in that. And I intend to question Luc about it tonight. I've told you before, we're pretty much impervious to their sort. They may try to wheedle us or force us into allowing possession, but they can't do much to us without our full consent."

"I wonder why that is."

"I haven't a clue. And I'm mostly taking Jude's word for it."

"It might be revealing to find out what happened to Natasha."

"I agree. But it won't be pleasant. Luc will be furious about being questioned." Then he sighed. "I feel like a caged tiger. I haven't felt that way often. The other time was when my great-granddaughter was attacked. Now again, with you. I hate not being able to take charge and set you free of this threat."

"I don't think that's a failing on your part. We still don't know enough to act. Any of us."

"No, I realize that. And it's driving me nuts because I feel there was something in that book Avi gave me, something I read but didn't quite get. I need to think more about it. I absolutely loathe the sense that something important is escaping me."

She nodded. Then she did something very daring, and possibly very stupid. She leaned to the side until she rested against his shoulder and arm. Tense, she waited for rejection. Instead, after a moment, his arm wound around her shoulders and drew her comfortably to his side. She relaxed into him, glorying in being so close, and delighting in the fact that he no longer seemed quite so reluctant to be near to her.

He spoke again. "Much of what people assume about angels is apparently false."

"How so?"

"Well, we call them messengers from God, we imagine they're perfect in every way, and assume that they're basically one-dimensional. If what I read earlier is any indication, they're every bit as complex as we are, and equally prone to fault. They have arguments, they have wars, they mated with human women…"

"Wait. Why would they want to do that? That troubles me. They're so different from us. It's like King Kong falling in love with Fay Wray."

He chuckled quietly. "As I said, they're not so very different from us. They're actually…" He paused, looking struck. A second or two later he said, "Like us."

He jumped up without further explanation and went to Jude's office. He didn't even knock, just threw the door open.

"Jude. What if Asmodai is like us? Vampires?"

Silence emanated from Jude's office. All of sudden he was in the front room with them and Creed had turned in the doorway to look at him. Yvonne closed her eyes and looked again, even though she should be getting used to this by now.

"What are you talking about?" she demanded. Neither of them answered. They were locked in stares, looking almost frozen.

"That," Jude said finally, "could be very interesting."

"It could be the key."

"What," Yvonne demanded again, "are you talking about?"

"We have huge appetites," Creed said. "Far beyond what we knew as mortals."

"Huge and hard to control," Jude agreed.

Creed looked at Yvonne. "I told you that you couldn't begin to imagine the kind of craving I feel for you. You offer me things which, gotten any other way, are merely poor substitutes. I live a life of cravings that are barely satisfied, a life of intense experience that makes me continue even when it all feels so pointless. Now imagine if I were to unchain those cravings. Give in to them. I—any vampire—could become such a horror that your kind would live in a state of terror and shock for a long time to come."

Yvonne felt her heart skitter. She'd had only a taste of what this man could do, and it was enough to make her quail at the thought of him dropping all his civilized rules.

"Exactly," Creed said, reading her response.

He turned back to Jude. "Suppose Asmodai is like us, plagued by such huge cravings, ones he can't satisfy in his own realm. Imagine that humans offer him, just as they offer us, a satisfaction he can't get anywhere else."

Jude again perched on the corner of Chloe's desk. "The one time we encountered a demon that truly wanted to master a vampire, it was only so he could gain our powers to destroy."

"Not to destroy. He wouldn't think of it that way. He'd think of it as slaking his need. For human blood, human sex, whatever. Destruction could be the byproduct."

"Right."

"And we have evidence from the Bible and other ancient sources that angels have fallen prey to the desire for human women."

"Indeed." Jude looked thoughtful. "That would explain the why of it, but we still need a solution."

"I don't deny that," Creed said, "but understanding Asmodai's motivation for all of this will help. It seems to me that they have supernatural powers much in the way we appear to. Perhaps some of those powers are augmented here, or perhaps some of them arise from persuasion. After all, we have the Voice."

"True. Are you trying to say they're not as dangerous as we think?"

"I'm not sure. I'm just trying to take a different angle of approach. If we can put them into better perspective, we may find it easier to figure out what we need to do."

Jude nodded. "Well, it would kind of fit." He gave a short laugh. "How many times in literature have we been referred to as dark angels? Perhaps they're our equivalent in another realm."

"Not an equivalent," Creed said, "but a kind of mirror image."

"But not all of you are bad," Yvonne remarked. "And angels have been known to do good things."

"Exactly," said Creed. "That's what I'm pondering here. A rogue angel. One who can probably satisfy his lusts a lot better here than he can in his own realm. But that means, like us, he can probably be killed or bound."

"You said Raphael bound him once. Can't we just call on another angel?"

Both Creed and Jude shook their heads simultaneously. "We're trying to *close* a gateway," Jude said.

"Precisely," Creed agreed. "The last thing we want to do is open yet another one. There's no way to be sure what might come through."

Yvonne could see that, but wondered privately if they weren't just going in circles here. What did it matter what kind of being Asmodai was? All that mattered was that they could send him back or destroy him.

Chloe interrupted further cogitation by returning with supper in the form of large salads and sandwiches. Only when Yvonne started eating did she realize just how famished she was.

She looked at Chloe. "You're right. They need to learn to take care of us."

Chloe snickered but Creed was suddenly there, touching her shoulder. "I'm sorry. Truly. It's been a long time since I've had to think about feeding a human."

"No," Chloe retorted, "all you think about is feeding *on* us."

Yvonne felt a giggle bubble up from her stomach. She tried to stop it, but it escaped anyway. The response was probably augmented by a touch of hysteria, she thought. Or reaction to fear. Because she wasn't sure she really felt like laughing right now. It just happened.

"Ouch," said Creed.

She looked up at him, still grinning from her laughter. "Did I say I minded?"

His golden eyes creased with a smile. "I don't recall it if you did."

"Too much info," Chloe announced, although she sounded as if she were joking.

Yvonne turned to her. "You have such a mouth, Chloe. I wish I could come up with that stuff off the cuff."

"Please no," both vampires said at once.

"One of me is enough," Chloe said smugly.

"I keep them on their toes. And you'll notice it's not *me* they fall in love with."

Yvonne's heart almost stopped. Surely she didn't mean Creed was falling in love with her. Certainly not. She must be referring to Jude and Terri.

But she felt a flicker of hope leap in her heart anyway, only to see it killed when she felt Creed stiffen beside her. He didn't like the implication at all.

But before she could fully tumble into the despair of wanting something she could never have, Jude spoke, defusing the moment.

"Some day your vampire will come."

In spite of her dismay, Yvonne had to laugh. She watched Chloe screw up her nose at Jude, but just then a buzzer rang. Chloe immediately looked at her monitor.

"Speak of the devil," she said, and pressed a button. "Luc is here. And no, he's not *my* vampire. I wouldn't have him if he crawled on his knees and came wrapped in a red ribbon."

"That's an image," Creed murmured, and Yvonne looked up to find him smiling at her. "Go on with your dinner," he added. "Chloe's right. I haven't been taking very good care of you."

She repositioned her chair, though, so that she could better keep an eye on Luc when he entered the office. She didn't trust him, not one bit.

He seemed completely subdued, and took a seat as far from Chloe and her as he could. In fact, he didn't look well, thought Yvonne as she forced herself to meet his black eyes. If it was possible to tell with a vampire, he looked awful. Exhausted.

Creed and Jude placed themselves on seats between him and Chloe, offering silent protection to the women.

"So," Luc asked, "what's the plan?"

"We don't have one yet," Creed responded. "We have Garner doing some research, and we're doing some of our own. And we have questions for you."

"Me? I know nothing about this Asmodai."

"But," said Creed, leaning toward him, "you know something we don't."

"That is?"

"How Natasha got into so much trouble with him. Most of the time demons avoid us."

If it were possible for a vampire to grow any paler, Luc did. His face tightened. "It's none of your business."

"It's our business now," Creed said forcefully. "A woman, *my lady* as you referred to her, is at risk. And now we're all at risk because Asmodai knows we've joined forces. We need every bit of information we can get. So tell me, Luc, how was it Natasha tangled with him?"

Luc let out a deafening roar. Yvonne covered her ears and very nearly dove under Chloe's desk, expecting an attack of some kind. But if that was Luc's intent, the next thing she saw was Creed and Luc standing face to face, and Creed's hand pressed hard against Luc's chest.

"Don't try anything," Creed said in a voice so deep and echoing it didn't sound human. "There are two of us to stop you."

Luc's lips pulled back from his teeth, his eyes seemed to grow even blacker, but then he shoved Creed's hand away, almost too quickly to see, and fell back on the chair. "Cut off my head," he snarled. "It would be easier."

"Yes," Creed agreed, "it probably would. For you. I thought you wanted vengeance."

"I do!"

"Then tell us what we need to know."

For long minutes, the office was absolutely silent. Yvonne watched, torn between fear and fascination. Luc put his face in his hand and sat motionless for what seemed like forever. When he looked up at last, his face had grown smooth. Expressionless.

"She wanted to give me a gift," he said in a monotone. "For some reason she thought it would please me if she became human again, so I could drink from her and know that particular sweetness again. It would *not* have pleased me, but I didn't know her plan until it was too late. I don't know how she summoned him, or what deal she might have made. I just know that when she came to me again, she was human and possessed both. I refused to drink from her, and demanded we find an exorcist. I thought if we could get rid of the demon, I could turn her once more."

"No?" Creed asked gently.

Luc shook his head. "I didn't have time to find out. Her last words to me were, 'I have been betrayed.' Then she ran out onto our balcony and jumped to her death."

Even feeling such distaste for Luc after the

way he had treated her, Yvonne felt a huge rush of sympathy. "I am so, so sorry," she said softly.

Those dark eyes came to her face. "I believe you, madam. But I question which of us she felt had betrayed her, the demon or me."

"The demon obviously," Yvonne said firmly. She might not know a lot about vampires, but she knew something about women. "How could you think anything else? She wouldn't want you to blame yourself for what she did, and what that thing did to her."

"So certain?" he asked with a mirthless half smile. "I wish I were."

"I think it's obvious," Yvonne told him. "She wanted to give you a gift, a gift that she knew would eventually mean she had to go through the change again. And I hear that's a terrible process."

"It is," Luc agreed. Something in his drawn face softened. "Perhaps."

"All right," said Creed, motioning Luc to resume his seat. "We know what happened in the end. The question is how she got there. Demons are good at planting thoughts and desires."

"Not so much in vampires," Jude argued.

"Not the way they attack humans. But when it comes to us they have different methods, don't they. Look at the one that used Terri to get you to give permission for a possession. If you'd been less strong, it might have succeeded. As it is, any number of people could have been used to plant the suggestion in Natasha's mind that this would be an ideal gift. Once again, these beings used love as a crowbar."

"Now *that,*" Jude said, "may be a very important observation."

"Only insofar as vampires are concerned."

Jude smiled crookedly. "And perhaps insofar as *you're* concerned."

Yvonne watched Creed go utterly still, that motionlessness she saw only from him, only from vampires. She thought she knew what Jude meant, and it embarrassed her. Creed plainly thought of her only as someone who needed protecting. Well, and as a sex object.

For the first time in her life, she realized she didn't object to being a sex object, certainly not where Creed was concerned. Feeling her cheeks heat, she gazed down at her plate to conceal her blush.

Luc made an impatient sound, and leaped to

his feet. "If you want me to cooperate, give me something to do."

Jude spoke. "Garner is looking for a musical band called Tommy and the Mechanics. His job is to make them think he's a talent scout and see if he can get close enough to find out if they have anything to do with Asmodeus. You could join him, since you recognize the stench so well."

"Why do you think they have anything to do with this?"

"Because Yvonne used to date Tommy and he's desperate for fame and fortune. He might have offered her up as a prize."

Luc's bleak gaze returned to Yvonne. "It would hardly be surprising. If love makes us do strange things, scorned love make us do even stranger ones. Very well. I will look and report back."

"On your way," Creed suggested, "could you sniff around my place? Asmodai was there earlier, and I'm not taking Yvonne back until we're sure he's gone."

"I will. I could smell that devil even through a closed door."

He vanished, his departure signaled only by the slamming of the street door.

"That was fun, wasn't it?" Chloe remarked. But her usual sarcastic attitude had given way to something that sounded far sadder. "Imagine thinking that doing something like that, that changing yourself, would make your lover happier."

"It's amazing," Creed agreed. "I wouldn't have thought Natasha insecure enough to fall for that."

"These demons are insidious," Jude said. "The thought probably never occurred to Natasha until it was planted. Very carefully planted and tended."

Perhaps, Yvonne thought, like the notion she kept getting to walk out on Creed so she wouldn't be a burden. What if that wasn't her own thought? She shivered, appalled by the mere notion.

Creed noticed. "Are you cold, Yvonne?"

"No. I'm fine. I'm just wondering how many of my own thoughts are actually my own. And," she added as another thought struck her, "what if I'm no longer the ultimate prize? What if I've become the means to another end?"

"Don't even think that." Creed astonished her by lifting her from her chair, carrying her to the couch—at a blessedly human pace for once—then sitting with her on his lap. He didn't seem to care what anyone thought.

He tucked her head against his shoulder, just beneath his chin. "Don't start having these thoughts. Fears and worries will weaken you. And honestly, I can take care of myself."

She sighed, forcing herself to let go of the fearful thoughts, at least for now, and allowed herself to enjoy being held. She should have felt embarrassed, with Jude and Chloe there, but she was getting past all of that.

All she wanted was to be close to Creed.

Creed's phone rang and he shifted her a bit so he could pull it out of his pocket. "Yes? Thanks, Luc. Later." He disconnected and spoke to Jude. "No sign of Asmodai at my place right now."

"Good. Then let me go back there with you and ward the place."

Everything moved swiftly then. Creed got her buttoned into her coat. Chloe offered her a muffler to protect her face, pointing out that Jude could bring it back.

Soon she was racing along streets and over rooftops on Creed's back again.

Only when they were inside Creed's condo did things slow down enough for her to see what was going on. Jude was already marking doors, walls and windows with holy oil.

Then he came over to her and used his thumb to dab some on her forehead. Even Creed submitted to the marking.

"Okay," Jude said. "Now we wait. I'll call you if I learn anything. You do the same."

Unencumbered by any mortals, Jude took his leave by way of the balcony, vanishing instantly into the night.

"I hate this," Yvonne said frankly.

Creed immediately appeared beside her on the couch. "What?"

"This waiting. Not knowing. Everything on hold. What if Tommy has nothing to do with this? What if Garner is just wasting his time?"

"It's possible. But there are other ways to solve this mess."

She turned to look at him. "And this thing about being like vampires. How does that help?"

"If you understand motivation, you understand better what to expect. Besides, we can be killed, enslaved and manipulated, too. It's just harder to do it to us than to a human. But mainly, it changes our thinking."

"In what way?"

"Maybe we're not facing some insurmountable force at all."

"I'd like to believe that." She sighed, and Creed surprised her by once again slipping his arm around her. Apparently his aversion to being close was turning into something else. Something she liked.

"Creed?"

"Yes?"

"Why can't we? Why can't we just…be together. I promise not to chase after you for the rest of my life. I promise not to go vampire hunting in sleazy clubs." She shuddered a little. "Honestly, I don't think anything could make me do that."

"Maybe not. There are always exceptions." But he sounded dubious.

She looked at him again, tipping her head back. He was looking straight at her, and she glimpsed strain in his face. *That's* what she was making him feel. A terrible tension between his needs and his desire to do the right thing.

"I hate myself!" She jumped up and stormed across the room to look out the windows.

"Why? What brought that on?"

"I'm driving you nuts. I'm being selfish. You're just trying to be decent and take care of me, and all I do is make you suffer."

"Ah, but such sweet suffering." He was there without warning, tipping her face up with his finger, looking deep into her eyes. "I was troubled at first, mainly because I feared testing my self-control."

"Well, you get an A on that test."

"Do I? Do I even want one at this point?" He gave a short laugh. "I told you this was playing with fire. How close to the flames do you want to dance? Because the way I'm feeling right now, I'd walk right into them."

She sucked in a deep breath, going utterly still. Her insides ached with the force of longing. Then, quietly, "I'm provoking you again. I'm sorry."

"You provoke me with every breath you draw. Every step you take. Every smile, every frown, every word. You can try to stop, but it won't make any difference. I want you with a hunger you can't begin to imagine. You don't have to do a damn thing except exist. And don't even suggest leaving. I won't let you out of my sight."

"Creed, I'm sorry."

"Don't be." A smile began to lift the corners of his mouth. "There's something to be said for defying temptation."

"Yeah? What?" She suddenly felt grumpy.

"That it's sweet beyond belief when you finally give in."

She gasped, whether from shock or delight she didn't know. His arms enclosed her snugly, and the next thing she knew, she was lying on the bed beside him, locked into his cocoon of forever darkness. She felt him stir, then the dim bedside lamp turned on.

"If you want to object," he murmured, "now would be a good time. Otherwise I'm going to dance with you to the very edge of the fire."

Her heart slammed, then began a rapid tattoo. "Creed, are you sure?"

"No." He laughed quietly. "Neither are you. But we're going to find out unless you choose otherwise, right this instant."

Looking into his eyes, recognizing heat and hunger that at least matched her own desire, she could barely get out one word. "Yes."

The holy oils held it back, keeping it from entering, but it could still hear. And what it had heard made it want to laugh. So they thought they could keep him out. So the undead called Creed thought he could protect her.

Little did they know, but just as they could bar his entry with Chrism, he had found a way to bar theirs. Once his circle was formed, only Yvonne would be able to enter it. The undead would become useless to her.

And he was going to enjoy possessing her so much more because Creed wanted her, too. Ah, this was entertainment beyond his hopes when he had set his plan in motion.

Satisfied, it withdrew to attend other matters. Tomorrow night, it would have what it wanted, and the one called Creed would be so devastated he would probably take his own life.

Now that would be a delicious fillip indeed.

Chapter 10

Creed gave himself one last moment of sane thought, but it wasn't enough to save him. He had already crossed one line this morning by drinking from this woman, and he had stopped in time. Well, there were other pleasures he could give her, pleasures that would thrill them both without taking her too far.

He knew the point at which to stop. He mustn't drink from her while they climaxed. At that point a bonding would take place, in her at least, that would be unshakable. He suspected the same would happen to him.

For if ever he had been in danger of a claiming, he knew it was now.

So he had to stop, and he would stop, but neither of them could go on like this much longer. Every time she looked at him he could read the longing and hunger in her gaze. He could smell it all around her when they were alone. She expressed no interest of any kind in another vampire so he was certain what she felt was no mere fascination.

But he didn't know what he felt except a longing, a hunger, a need beyond any he had felt before, and it was maddening him.

With all that loomed before them, possibly death or worse, he couldn't justify the fight any longer. Asmodai had come here to find her. They probably had only hours left, and at any moment Asmodai might return.

And despite all his bravado about being able to protect her, he wasn't at all certain of that. Not against a creature like this one.

So he accepted her yes and his own yearnings and gave in. He kissed her as mortals kiss, reveling in the warmth of her mouth and tongue, in the way she arched into him and wound her arms around him. The scent of her desire perfumed the air, an aphrodisiac unlike any other. And because he had already drunk from her, even that tiny bit, he felt the synchrony begin. Two minds, one body.

This was not his first such experience. In the months after his change, before he had learned self-control, he had experienced this many times. Those memories had shamed him for so long, keeping him isolated. But this time he was sure he could stop himself before carrying her too far.

And this time he could not deny himself, not when she so clearly wanted him, not when one of them might be gone soon.

If, in the end, either of them were left alone, they would at least have the memory.

And memory, he had learned, was the most important part of existence. Without it, nothing had meaning. Nothing at all.

He sipped from her lips, his heart hammering exactly in time with hers. He felt her nerve endings excite with passion, and his own responded in kind. Heady bliss filled him along with driving hunger.

He cast thought aside, descending into the

essential nature of his being: wanting, needing, feeling, experiencing. Totally in the now.

He craved every warm silken inch of her. For him, removing her clothes was scant impediment. He had them off her, had her naked beside him, almost before she knew it.

Her eyes had turned hazy with need, but a small smile curved her lips as she realized what he had done. An instant later his own clothes had vanished, and he gathered her close, reveling in her soft curves, her warm skin, the throb of her sweet blood through her entire being. Wherever she touched him, he felt heat, long-missed heat. That alone, for him, approached ecstasy.

But he knew she needed more, so much more, and he was determined to give her as much as he safely could.

With the thunder of blood in his ears, he began to taste her, trailing his lips and tongue over her. *That* was an intimacy he had never shared with anyone, not even his wife. Never before had he felt a desire to learn a woman with more than his hands.

But this one was different in so many ways. He needed the taste of her as much as the feel of her. When his tongue at last reached her breast, her shudders of pleasure gave way to a cry of delight. Ever so gently he caught her nipple between his teeth, biting, not enough to break her skin, but enough to catch her on that incredible arc between pleasure and pain. When she grabbed his head, holding him there, he knew an instant of triumph. Little nibbles followed by sucking, teasing her and tormenting them both with his every move. When he felt her nails rake his back, as if she could take no more, delight exploded in him.

He settled into a rhythm as he sucked and nipped until at last her hips moved in time to his mouth.

She was his, and the knowledge of his power, of the pleasure he gave them both, filled him like a hot tide, racing through him from head to foot.

His own body began to move with hers, just as his heart pounded with hers, as his breaths echoed hers. In these moments, the prison of solitude that had held him for a hundred years vanished. *Not alone.* No sweeter feeling existed…

Except for the passion that drove him. The

passion to pleasure, the passion to possess, the passion to reach the pinnacle of joyous sensation.

His member ached, throbbing in time to their hearts, and he pressed it hard against her smooth belly, seeking a release he wouldn't grant himself. Not this time.

"Creed..." Her voice ached as she called his name. At last he moved on with his explorations, but this time with his hand. Sliding his fingers between her legs, he parted her dewy petals and touched that bundled knot of nerves.

Another cry escaped her, and she arched, clamping her legs around his hand.

Oh, yes.

He kept stroking her there, stilling whenever she seemed about to crest, dragging out the agony, preventing the fulfillment as long as he could. He drew his tongue over her midriff and belly, making her shiver even more wildly, and feeling himself shudder in response.

He knew where she was, because he was there with her, teetering on that peak of utter, perfect pleasure.

He needed to bite her, to fill his mouth with the hot sweet taste of her life, and just at the moment he thought he would no longer be able to resist his own Hunger, he took her over the peak, riding the crest with her.

Just in time to save them both.

Yvonne felt shattered. Delightfully shattered. Curled in Creed's arms, she floated back to earth, feeling dazzled, feeling as if every nerve in her body had turned into a sparkler, sizzling with immense pleasure. Nothing, absolutely nothing, could compare with what had just happened. She'd had no idea she was capable of such overpowering physical sensation and delight.

Slowly, however, as thought began to emerge from the fog of feeling, she realized something.

"What about you?" she asked.

"What about me?"

"You gave me everything and I gave you nothing."

He smiled, looking unusually drowsy, and brushed a strand of hair back from her cheek. "You gave me everything. You gave me your experience."

"I don't..."

He laid a finger over her lips. "I drank from

you earlier. We're linked now, and your every feeling is mine when we make love. I was there with you, all the way."

"Wow," she whispered.

"Awesome," he replied, his eyes dancing. "Trust me, this is one part of being a vampire that I wouldn't exchange for anything."

"Is it like this between two vampires, too?"

His brow knit. "Why do you ask?"

"Because of what Luc said about Natasha wanting to be human again for him. She must have felt he was lacking something."

"That's a good question. From my own experience, admittedly limited, and what others have told me, the experience is every bit as intense between two vampires. Maybe *she* was the one who felt a lack. It's every bit as good, it's just a little different."

"Different how?"

"I wouldn't have felt your warmth. That's the only thing that wouldn't have been there."

"But you say you miss that."

"Sometimes. But I've lived a long time without it. I certainly don't miss it enough to have wanted my mate to do what Natasha tried to do. There are things I can't share with a mortal, things that in their own way make up for that one little lack. No, Natasha's decision really doesn't make sense to me."

"So somehow she was influenced?"

"That would be my guess."

Yvonne sighed, tucking her head into his shoulder, reveling in the new freedom that allowed her to do so. Never before had she been so aware of the walls that existed until the point of intimacy was reached. All need for pretense was gone. But maybe it had been gone for a while, since he could read her so well.

"I loved dancing near the fire," she told him.

"I did, too."

She refused to share the nascent hope in her heart though, that maybe someday they could dance right into the flames. For now she had to be content with the lines he drew, had to accept that he knew what was best for them both.

But as fabulous as their lovemaking had been, she was quite sure that something important had been left out.

Later, dressed in a loose jogging suit, she made coffee in the kitchen while Creed sat at his desk doing more research. "The key is here somewhere," he told her before he disappeared into dusty volumes.

Without warning, Garner arrived and Creed let him in. The young man appeared moderately agitated and insisted on pacing.

"I found this Tommy Sincks and his band. The stench was all over him and what's more, it's on a couple of members of his band. I didn't realize I'd already sniffed one of them out. Tommy's the nexus, all right." He glanced at Yvonne. "And you were right, too. Tone-deaf would be a generous description of him. I can't imagine how you put up with him."

"Sometimes," Creed said, "we all make less than brilliant choices for love. Get on with your story."

"What story? I told him I was a scout, gave him my card, and he told me he wasn't interested, that he had a deal in the pipeline."

"And?"

Garner shrugged. "I suggested he call me if the deal didn't pan out for him. He said he'd know in two days."

Creed looked at Yvonne. "That doesn't give us much time."

"No, but it gives us a time frame," Garner

said. "I called Jude a little while ago, but he didn't answer his phone. I swear, there's nothing as useless as a couple of new lovebirds. Anyway, sum and substance, Tommy thinks he's going to have the deal of his dreams in about forty-eight hours, he reeks of Asmodai, and his music stinks so bad only zombies could listen to it. There's no way he has a legit deal coming down."

"Anything else?" Creed asked.

Garner paused in his pacing. "Actually, yeah. I asked him who he was talking to. You know, as if I know everyone in the business."

"And?"

"He wouldn't say. But he did say he'd found a way to sweeten the deal, probably something I wouldn't be interested in."

Creed sat up straighter. "He'd sweeten the deal?"

"His words." And Garner looked straight at Yvonne. "I suspect you're the sweetener. And while I may not know a thing about the record business, I'm fairly certain you can't get anywhere by bribing a talent scout or a producer. It's expensive to record and put an album out, and there's no way Tommy could have anything big enough to sweeten that kind of deal with a legitimate company."

"He barely has enough to scrape by himself," Yvonne agreed. Her head whirled though, as she realized she hadn't wanted to believe this about Tommy. Even when it had been discussed, a big part of her had listened in disbelief. This was a man she had been in love with, a man she had shared her life, her bed, her home with. To think that he would use her as a pawn…

A shudder ripped through her. No, he would. All of sudden she was certain of it. As new pieces of her image of Tommy slammed into place, she became convinced that he was more than a cheater. He was a guy who would do anything to get what he wanted.

"So," Creed said to Garner, "how many have we got for the circle now?"

"Depends on how it has to be drawn. If it includes Tommy, then we've got five. If he's not part of the circle, we still need one more."

Creed looked down at the books he'd been reading, touching one of them with his hand. "We probably need to find one more. From what I've been reading—and I'm assuming it's correct—someone apart from the circle has to perform the invocation and the sacrifice."

"So one more." Garner rubbed his face. "He could be intending to get another of his band members involved at the last minute. Regardless, I need to get out there again. Let Jude know what I found out if he ever surfaces."

Creed let him out, locking the door behind him. Then he faced Yvonne, and she saw the creases of worry on his face.

Her hands knotted and she tried to think of something reassuring to say, not that she felt very reassured herself. "Nothing's changed," she said finally. "Except now we know who's at the center of all this. He still needs to get one more person."

"And we have a time frame. Not much time at all."

She sat there, thinking about what she had just learned, about what it might mean. The more she thought, the more panicky she felt, because there was no way she could see that she wasn't boxed in.

"Yvonne?" Creed squatted in front of her, taking her hands. "Yvonne, what's wrong? I can smell your terror."

She looked at him, sorrow lodging in her throat alongside her fear. There could be no happy ending here, no matter how she looked at it. Even if she survived this, it was clear Creed wouldn't want her around for long, because he feared going too far with her, feared coming to loathe himself for following his natural urges.

A short time ago she couldn't have even begun to imagine such a conflict, at least not to the degree that Creed was experiencing. To him what she offered was like food and drink, and she couldn't imagine having to deny yourself that when you were starving. Or to have a moral conflict over so much as sampling a feast laid out for you.

"Creed," she said finally around the lump in her throat, "I'm going crazy."

"What?" His hands tightened on hers. "What makes you say that?"

"This is intolerable. You need to get rid of me as soon as possible. I'm just a constant torment. And then there's this thing Tommy unleashed. What if it hurts you, or Jude, or Chloe and Garner? I couldn't stand it."

"We'll take care of it. And I'm not in any rush to get rid of you."

Sighing, she tugged a hand free and cupped his cheek. "I make you want things you don't dare take, things that you'll feel bad about taking if you do."

"Yvonne..."

"Let me finish, please. So far I've been little but baggage around here. Someone to be constantly cared for but who offers nothing at all. I even, stupidly, got you into a fight with Luc when I tried to run. I could have gotten you killed!"

He started to speak, but she moved her thumb just enough to cover his lips. She could feel the tension in him, but he held the words back.

"However this goes down," she continued, "whatever happens, there's only one path to the end of this road and I know it."

"Meaning?" His breath felt cool against her thumb.

"I'm the bait. You can't protect me every second. Before Tommy goes ahead with whatever he's planning, if I'm the so-called sweetener, he's going to need to get to me. He can't do that if I'm hiding behind a protective wall of vampires."

She saw it in his expression, the knowledge that she was right. But then his face twisted, he jumped up, and let out a deafening roar. She almost clapped her hands over her ears, but the sound died so quickly she didn't have time.

"Creed?"

He vanished and reappeared on the far side of the room. An instant later he was in the kitchen. Then he was once again in front of her, pulling her up into his arms, holding her so tight she could barely breathe.

"Creed?" she gasped.

He loosened his hold just enough to let her breathe. "Do you think," he asked tightly, "can you possibly think, I want to risk you that way? I'd rather walk into the fires of hell."

She tipped her head enough to see his face. "I believe you," she said quietly. "I believe you. But there's no other way and you know it. Tommy has to be able to take me where he wants me. And I need to start setting it up."

"I want to talk to Jude first."

"What good will that do? Everyone knows, or at least seems to, that it won't be enough just to break the circle. Asmodai can just get Tommy to make another one. So we need a solution, and from what I've been hearing, that demon at least needs to start emerging into this world. Then…then, I don't know what you need to do. But you'll never get an opportunity and none of us will be safe if we don't deal with this once and for all."

"I should just go kill Tommy right now."

She could tell he meant it, and for an instant an icy feeling trickled along her spine. But she knew what he was, and the momentary shock didn't last long. Especially given the situation they were in. That was no cold-blooded threat. "How long will that hold off Asmodai? And how will you feel if he finds another means to come through and you don't know about it because he's doing it to someone else? How will you feel when you learn there have been other victims?"

His face seemed to darken, his eyes grew blacker than coal. In those moments she saw why his kind were sometimes referred to as Lords of the Night. He seemed, somehow, to become part of the darkness right before her eyes.

Then he said something that caused her heart to stutter. "We don't weep, my kind."

"What?"

"You don't know what a mercy tears can be until you can't shed them. And because we can't weep, we get angry. You see Luc. His rage comes from a pain he can show no other way."

Her throat tightened again. "I'm sorry."

"Don't be. It's the way we are. Yvonne, you need to understand just how different we are from you."

"I'm beginning to." Confusion caused her to furrow her brow. "What are you trying to say?"

"Don't protect me. I'm not worth it. On the other hand, I don't want anything to happen to you. If anything does, I'll shred this world in my fury."

"Because you can't weep?"

"In part."

"But I think you're worth protecting."

"And that shows how little you really know about me and my kind. What you've seen has been a veneer. You never saw me stalk innocents down dark alleys when I was young and out of control. You never saw me take a life to slake my own cravings. You don't know what I can be."

"I know what you are now."

He shook his head, then released her suddenly, reappearing across the room. "You see what I try to be, not what I *am*."

"What you *try* to be is all that counts. Because all any of us can do is try to be better than what we are. Even we humans need to fight that battle."

His smile was crooked and humorless. "You make it sound so simple."

"It really *is* that simple," she argued. "Creed, you have to stop beating yourself up. I may not be a hundred years old, but I know some things, and one of them is that as long as you're trying your best, you're being the best you can be. You think I haven't noticed how you live in a constant state of deprivation because you feel you can't and shouldn't take the things you most need and want? Cripes, monks don't have it as hard. At least for them temptation isn't all around them."

All of sudden he relaxed and a laugh escaped him. "You might have a point. Regardless, I'm not going to put you in needless danger."

"Needless is the key word," she told him firmly. "And I honestly don't see how we can avoid it. I'll call Tommy tomorrow and tell him some lie about how I'm missing him."

Creed hesitated, then nodded. "That might get us a whole lot of information. Useful information."

"Well, if I don't call him, he's going to have to call me. He's got to get to me somehow."

"Let me think about this. And you need to tell me more about your breakup."

"Why?"

"Because I need to know whether it would be believable for you to call him."

At that she almost laughed. "You don't know Tommy's ego. He's probably absolutely convinced I'm in the process of trying to find a way to come back to him."

"I'm beginning to detest him, and I've never met him."

"Trust me, it's very lowering to think I ever thought I was in love with him."

"Some people present one face until they think they've got you. Then they show you an entirely different side," he remarked.

"He certainly changed. I don't know whether he was putting on a front at first, or if his friends really caused it. I often had the feeling that they brought out something in him I'd never suspected was there."

"They may have. Don't beat yourself up about it either way. You saw what he let you see."

"And you," she asked, feeling a twinge of nervousness, "am I seeing the real you?"

"You know I've been pretty blunt. There are parts of me I hope you never see, because they're parts of me I don't ever want to let out again."

She nodded. "I can deal with that. It's what we try to be that matters. I already told you that. What Tommy seemed to be trying to become in those last months, especially, was not something I admired."

"Well, don't admire me. I'm not admirable."

"And I disagree."

She watched something in his face change, but she couldn't read what was going on. If anything, he seemed to become more inscrutable. "What makes your eyes change?" she asked impulsively.

"My mood. Whether I've fed. If I get too hungry, too intense, too angry, my eyes tend to darken." He shrugged. "Call it my emotional barometer. See, now you have a way to read me, too."

"I like that." And she did. Reading him seemed to have become one of her major preoccupations.

"Just keep in mind," he said quietly, "that when my eyes are dark, I'm much more dangerous."

"Why?"

"Because I'm walking the edge between impulse and restraint. The very edge."

She absorbed that, taking it in and accepting it. "So it would be easier to tip the wrong way?"

"Infinitely easier. And everything inside me is pushing me to react to my basest urges."

"Maybe not all of them are base," she said quietly. "Maybe some of them are essential."

Creed slipped out onto the terrace to escape her scent again. Just for a few minutes. But it was getting hard, so hard, to control his desire for her. She had a view of things that he was tempted to call naive, but even as he wanted to dismiss her thoughts that way he knew what the real difference was: Yvonne was still hopeful. For himself he'd given up on those hopes a long time ago.

And that didn't make him feel very proud of himself.

He'd defined himself in the worst ways possible, never admitting the possibility that he might not be a monster. He had essentially hidden away from the world for a century because he feared what he had become during his change.

He'd found his way into an ivory tower of isolation where controlling his needs had been comparatively easy, and he'd never once considered that he had gifts that might be useful toward good ends.

He'd become a monk, and remembering what Yvonne had earlier said about monks having it easier than he did, he knew she was wrong. He'd made it as easy as possible on himself, hiding away, exposing himself to no test, nor any real possibility of a test.

He was, it seemed, afraid of failing. *Terrified* of failing. Unlike most, he knew what his failures could mean for others, but that still didn't excuse him for being a moral coward. He had told himself he was taking the high ground, sparing others the risk.

Instead he'd been sparing himself, probably more than anyone else.

Given what Yvonne had just offered to do, his own cowardice had never been clearer. Oh, he would die to protect her. He just didn't want to have to deal with the day-to-day temptations his Hunger awoke in him.

And dying, he admitted to himself, would be the easier task by far.

He sighed, then drew in a deep breath of the night air. He could smell the humans all around, hear their night sounds, their lovemaking. He could hear the cries of infants and the shouts of arguing couples. He could see all the colors of the rainbow in the night sky above, clouded though it was with light and pollution. He could feel the life of the city throbbing around him as if it were his own pulse beat.

Why did he deny himself so much? Why was he so certain he lacked control? Over these days with Yvonne he had certainly proved he had enough control.

He heard the door slide open behind him, caught the intoxicating fresh scent of her.

"Am I bothering you?" she asked quietly.

"No. Not at all."

She came closer, and he turned, reaching out with an arm to draw her close to his side.

"Is something wrong?"

"No, actually." He gave her a gentle squeeze, the gentlest he could manage, aware that it would be far too easy to crush her. "I was just having an epiphany."

"About what? If you don't mind me asking."

He gave a slight shake of his head. "You got me to thinking. You know Jude, you see what he's done with his existence since his change."

"Well, a little, yes."

"I took an entirely different route. Instead of engaging and finding a way to use my change to benefit others, I chose instead to hide away from all the temptation. I became that monk you were talking about."

"I didn't mean…"

"You may not have meant it to be about me, but you didn't know me before we met. I chose to hide, to simplify my life so that it wasn't a constant struggle against my instincts. I thought it was wise. Now I think it was selfish."

She tilted her head to better look at him, and he felt her arm slip around his waist and give him a squeeze. "You did what you thought best, and while I may not know much about your change, I suspect from what you said that it was a major trauma."

"Perhaps. But it's time for this vampire to grow up."

"What? You're already grown up."

"Not as grown up as I could be. I avoid the tests that this life gives me."

"Like what?"

"Like this." He moved swiftly, lowering his head until his mouth touched her throat. He licked her skin gently and listened to her draw a sharp breath of pleasure.

"Creed?"

"I can drink from you without harming you. I can love you without harming you. I can be around you without harming you. The only question is whether I'm willing to practice the restraint required."

He heard her heart skip, and the sound made him smile to himself. He licked her throat again and felt the shiver that ran through her.

"No," she said, on a mere wisp of breath, "there's another question."

"What's that?"

"Am I worth it for you to have to practice such restraint?"

"And," he added gently, "am I worth it to you to put up with all this crap I call a life?"

She drew a breath as if she would answer, but he laid a quick finger over her lips. "It's too soon," he said huskily. "Too soon to answer such questions. Especially when we face this threat."

He felt the resistance in her, but he was sure he was right about this one. She was dependent on him right now, much as she hated it, and it could affect her decisions. She had to be free to come and go as she chose before he could trust anything she might feel. Before *she* could trust herself.

Until then…

Until then there were some pleasures that could be safely taken, that had already been offered. Lifting her into his arms, he carried her back inside and sat on the couch with her on his lap.

"I like it when you carry me," she murmured, and there was that maddening blush again, making his pulse pound in his ears. "I never thought I'd like that."

"You're as light as feather down to me," he muttered, "and so much more delightful."

Seeing a reflection of his own hunger in her gaze, he tugged the neck of her shirt to one side and nosed around until he found a suitable vein. Then he licked her gently, numbing her, and extended his fangs, plunging them carefully into her. Just enough to taste, not enough to do harm.

At once she arched and moaned, and the incredible magic of vampire and victim began, leading them both along a path that was probably as close to heaven as he would ever know.

Chapter 11

"You may not want to build a temple," Avi Herschel said as he walked into Creed's condo the next evening, "but it may be the only way to skin the cat."

Creed stood to one side as Avi passed, then closed the door. "What do you mean?"

"I think you know what I mean."

Creed stood looking at him, then slowly nodded.

Yvonne, emerging from the bedroom, freshly showered, looked at the two of them. "He knows what?"

Creed turned to her. "Asmodai can't remove the Tetragrammaton himself."

"Precisely!" Avi beamed. Then he reached into a pocket and pulled out a large, flat wooden case. "This has history, my friend. I hate to part with it, but in the interests of saving your lady and keeping that demon bound…" He shrugged.

Yvonne hurried over in time to see Creed open the case and reveal a blackened chain loop with four strange characters woven into it. "Is that…?" She hardly dared say it.

"It is," said Avi. "Note that the characters are paleo-Hebrew. No one has written that since at least the first century, and I've had this much longer than that. I've kept it all these millennia in case. I guess this is *in case,* yes?"

"But how did it come off of him?" Creed asked. "If he can't remove it himself?"

"He cajoled one of his many concubines into doing it. However, since you plan to use it to send him back, he may not find it quite so easy to persuade someone in his own realm to remove it. You read the book I gave you?"

"Yes. It has even more power over his kind than us."

"So, it is safe to assume *they,* whoever they are, will not be quick to want to touch it. At least I hope not. If you remove it from one, it might be used to bind another. You see the conundrum his kind will face?"

Creed was nodding as he held up the roughly made necklace, turning it in the dim light. "Avi, to touch something this old, something that I always thought was myth…"

"I know, my friend. Just promise to use it wisely."

"I will."

"I would not give it to you otherwise. Now I return to my books. If I learn anything new, I will tell you."

Avi vanished instantly, the only mark of his passing the sound of the door closing and locking. Yvonne was fascinated by the necklace, and reached out to touch it with one finger.

"How old is this?" she asked.

"Can't be sure, but my guess is about three thousand years. Historians estimate that to be the approximate time the First Temple was built."

"I can't imagine," she breathed.

He lowered the necklace back into the box but didn't close the lid. There was something almost reverential in his handling of it. "I'm a historian," he remarked. "I've handled a lot of old things, especially since I move among vampires and a lot of us are very, very old. But nothing like this, ever. And its mere existence gives proof to myths that have persisted for millennia. This is…amazing."

"I agree." Once again she reached out to touch it with a fingertip.

"And now I have headache," he remarked wryly.

"What's that?"

"I must guard this necklace as closely as I guard you. If someone else were to get it…" He left the thought incomplete, simply shaking his head again. "Maybe I should just wear it."

"But what might it do to you?"

He shrugged. "I have no idea."

She grabbed his forearm. "Then don't even consider it," she begged. "It goes on one being, and one only. Maybe I should wear it."

"Then he'd never get close to you, that's for sure."

"And we'll never get rid of him. He'll just go elsewhere. You know that, Creed. We have to do this, and I have to call Tommy."

When he turned his head to look directly at her, she saw his eyes were black.

"Creed?"

"You've changed."

She felt taken aback for a few seconds, then understanding dawned. "No, I haven't. You're meeting the real me, Creed. I was just overwhelmed and confused at first. But I've never been a coward, and now that I'm starting to understand, and to see the path we have to take, I'm not afraid to take it. That's the way I've always been, whether you believe it or not."

One corner of his mouth lifted slowly. "I believe you. But a little fear is often a useful survival tool. Don't lose it all."

"I'm in no danger of that."

"Interesting," he murmured, looking at the box again.

"What is?"

"Religious scholars have debated for a long, long time whether Asmodai is a tool used to teach lessons. And look at the two of us. I'm emerging from nearly a century of stasis and you...well, you're prepared to face the unknown no matter what it holds rather than let Asmodai try his wiles elsewhere. Are we both growing from this? I know I am. I'm finding something more important than my desire for solitude and peace."

She nodded. "I think I'm learning, too. At some level I've lived in the world of my imagination. I look back at my relationship with Tommy, which I thought was me learning to live a real life, and what I see was that I was living in yet another world of my creating until he dashed all my fantasies."

He turned to face her. "And now?"

"Now I think I'm ready to take on life. And maybe death. But I'm not retreating into my safe little world this time."

He nodded. "Same here. And these are questions that we'll never get answered. We just have to soldier on. The grander scheme is seldom revealed to us."

His phone beeped and he pulled it out, quickly scanning a text message. "Jude is on his way. Can Luc be far behind?" He almost sighed.

"You think Luc is watching everything?"

"Probably. He's agreed to cooperate, but that doesn't mean he trusts us not to leave him out."

"I don't think I like him. But evidently you did once?"

"He was all right. I think I mentioned we cooperated on a problem, one of the few times I broke my self-imposed isolation over the years."

She gave him a small smile. "So you haven't always remained in your ivory tower?"

"Sometimes you just can't. Too much is at stake."

She sighed, touched the rough wooden box again, then sank onto the couch. "I've never had that kind of stake in anything in my life. I'm starting to feel very selfish."

"Why so?" He placed the box on the end table and sat beside her.

"Well, I've avoided involvement in a lot of ways. I think the biggest risk I ever took was submitting my first manuscript to a publisher. That turned out not to be such an awful risk at all because I didn't get the raft of rejection letters most new writers get. I didn't even get one. I was twenty-six and published. That's rare. And it gave me an excuse to bury myself even deeper."

"Sounds like me."

She shook her head. "No, it's not like you at all. You had a life before your change. A wife, five children, you were teaching. You got a lot more involved than I ever have. Me, I had to have a demon come after me to wake me up."

An almost gentle laugh escaped him. "Sleeping Beauty?"

"Hardly." She sighed. "Regardless of how I got there, I was well on my way to becoming a hermit. And I liked it. I've always been an introvert. I think what attracted me to Tommy was that he sparkled. Or seemed to at first. I was flattered when he noticed me, yes, but it was more than that. For a little while he filled out my life. For a little while I was doing all the things I'd avoided before. I was getting out in the world because he'd take me. To clubs, to movies, to parties. It was very different, and it was heady. For a while."

"I can understand that."

"Anyway, who I was then doesn't matter now. Now all that matters is Asmodai and making sure he doesn't hurt someone. And I'm being serious, Creed. Now that I've gotten over the shock and confusion, I know one thing for certain, and it's that this ceremony can't be allowed to happen. You said something about a sacrifice. Some poor person is going to be killed to further Tommy's ambitions? I don't think so."

"We're in definite agreement on that."

Before they could say any more, there was a tapping at the terrace sliding glass doors. Jude stood out there. Apparently, Yvonne thought, since he was unencumbered by humans, he'd arrived by a less traditional route. Part of her wondered just how neat it must be to do things like that.

Creed let him in. Jude seemed to emanate cold, probably from the chilly night. Of course, Yvonne thought, these vampires didn't make a whole lot of heat of their own.

After greeting them both, Jude leaned back against the dining table, crossed his legs at the ankle, and folded his arms. "I told Luc to meet us here in about half an hour. If he's watching, as I suspect he is, he'll probably arrive any minute to be sure he isn't missing something. As for Garner, he came up with a bit. Tommy called him earlier. Seems he wants to meet with Garner the day after tomorrow if his deal falls through."

"Garner told us."

"Two days. That means he's hoping to form the circle tomorrow night. Does he know how to get in touch with you, Yvonne?"

"I haven't changed my cell phone number. I don't know if he knows my address."

"I suspect he does." Jude waved a hand. "Chloe identified those things we found in your apartment. Two were designed to exercise influence over you. The other was more like an identifier, a beacon. My guess is that Tommy somehow got in there and placed them, maybe as you were in the process of moving in."

Yvonne wanted to protest, but as she recalled the day of her move-in, the way the door to her apartment had stood open for a few hours as the movers carried things in, and the number of times she had run downstairs to check on something, she knew it was possible. It was equally possible, as she had thought a few days ago, that Tommy could have wheedled a key from one of the movers. "I think you're right. There was plenty of time that day for him to slip in, plenty of time when the door was open. What surprises me is that he could have managed it without me seeing him at all."

"It didn't have to be him. He could have gotten one of the movers to do it, even slipped the stuff in with your belongings. Lots of ways around that. Regardless, he had your place marked at least from the moment you moved in."

"I think I want to kill him," Creed remarked so quietly the words were all the more chilling.

"It may come to that," Jude said bluntly. "People who are willing to go to these lengths to satisfy their desires are seldom to be trusted again. With any luck, though, we can scare him enough that he never wants to fool with the dark arts again."

"I guess I should call him," Yvonne said quietly. Her insides fluttered nervously, and she hoped it didn't show. "That's what he'd be expecting, since he put things in my apartment to influence me."

Jude looked at Creed. Creed nodded slowly. "We talked about it. She wants to do this."

"It would be a great help," Jude agreed. "Chances are, he'll set up a meeting. And it'll either happen there, or he'll take her to a place."

"Far more reliable," Creed said heavily,

"than hoping Garner can track it down in the time we have left."

Yvonne's hands clenched and she closed her eyes for a moment.

"You don't *have* to do this," Creed said.

"Yes. Yes I do. Whatever happens, if I survive, I'd like to be able to live with myself when it's over."

Rising, she walked down the hall to the empty bedroom where she had stored her suitcase and her purse. Her legs felt shaky, almost rubbery, and she wondered if she dreaded talking to Tommy that much. Or if she was dreading something else more.

One way or another, this had to end, and end quickly. She couldn't live in fear indefinitely. Even less could she stand being with Creed only because he felt he had to protect her. Yes, she hoped he wanted more from her, but if not, it needed to end now.

Because with each passing hour she was coming to care more for him. And right now, that was beginning to scare her as much as anything.

Back out in the living room, she sat near Creed and punched in Tommy's phone number. “He won’t answer the first time I call,” she warned them.

“Why not?” Creed asked.

“He never does. I think it’s an ego thing. He likes making people wait. So I just don’t leave messages, because that annoys him.”

Creed smiled crookedly. “Interesting dynamic.”

Yvonne disconnected and screwed up her nose. “The thing I wound up hating most, as much as him cheating on me, was when I realized I was becoming just as petty as he was.”

Creed reached out and touched her cheek with cool fingertips. “You’re not the petty type.”

“I used to think so. Now I’m not so sure.” She put her phone on the end table. “I need to make him wait about half an hour.”

“Hell,” Jude said. “How old is he? Six?”

Any other time, she might have smiled at the description. Right now, however, she was too nervous. Almost unconsciously her fingers strayed to the tiny scabs that Creed had left behind when he drank from her. Hidden by her shirt, no one else could see them, but she felt them.

And a shiver of shock ran through her. What was she doing? Falling in love with a *vampire?* Part of her mind rebelled instantly, screaming that such beings didn't exist. Yet she knew for a fact they did. She'd had too much experience of what they could do to doubt it. And yet some corner of her mind still wanted to dive into denial. And not just about vampires. About everything else, too, from Asmodai, and demons to ancient necklaces and…

Good God, how had she become involved in all this insanity?

And worse, how had she come to believe it wasn't insanity? Everything she knew about the world shrieked this couldn't be. Yet here she was, sitting with two vampires and proposing to make a date with a demon.

Startling her, her phone rang. With a hand that suddenly wanted to tremble, she reached for it and looked. "Tommy," she said.

"I guess," Creed drawled, "he's a little too concerned to make you wait a half hour."

That scared her. That, as much as anything anyone had suspected or said, told her Tommy was in this up to his neck. That he was conceivably willing to make her part of a deal with a demon. *That's* what he thought of her.

And no matter how much her rational mind might strike out at the thought that all this was real, she knew one thing for certain: Tommy thought it was real. And he was willing to trade her like a piece of goods.

"Hello," she said, trying to unclench her teeth.

"Vonnie," he said, almost but not quite sounding as he had long ago when he'd actually pretended to love her. "Man, it's good to hear your voice!"

At least that wasn't a lie, she thought with an unusually bitter reaction. He was probably as relieved as hell to hear from her if what they all suspected was true.

"You miss me?" he asked. The wheedling tone was familiar, too. Once she had thought it was cute.

It took her a moment, but she managed to say, "I thought we should talk. I left in a hurry. Maybe we can sort some stuff out."

"I'd like that," he said. "I'd really like that. I know I was a bastard doing what I did with Ellen. Jeez, Vonnie..."

Her mouth soured at the sound of the fake apology. “Look, save it,” she said. “I just think we need to settle some stuff, okay?”

“I agree.” And too quickly. Her stomach felt as if it flipped.

“So how about Arne’s?” she suggested, mentioning a place he liked to have a few beers.

“No, I don’t go there much anymore. I have a better idea. There’s this new club on Forty-Ninth, called The Far Place. Been there?”

“No.” She didn’t go clubbing anymore. She hadn’t before Tommy, and she didn’t after Tommy.

“You’ll like it,” he said, wheedling again. “I think it’s more your type of place. Quieter. Anyway, how about tomorrow night? I have a show first, so it would have to be about midnight. Can you make it?”

She wanted to tell him to shove it all into some dark hole. Instead she swallowed hard and looked from Creed to Jude. “Tomorrow night?”

“Yeah,” Tommy said. “I can’t wait to see you.”

Both Jude and Creed nodded agreement.

“All right,” Yvonne said. “Tomorrow night. Midnight. But you’d better not be late.”

"I won't be," Tommy hastened to say. "I've only got one set tomorrow. I'll be there."

When she hung up, she realized she was shaking internally, as if every nerve ending in her body were trying to crawl out of her.

"The Far Place," she said.

"We heard," Creed answered.

Shock shook her again. They'd heard? Then she realized that their speed and strength probably weren't the only supernatural things about them. Hyper acute hearing, too. She should have guessed.

Creed watched her with concern. She had changed in the time between her call to Tommy and his return call. Not much had shown on her face, but he didn't need her face to speak to him. He could smell the transformation in her, the building stress, the doubts, the sudden fears, even the temblor of shock.

The problem was, he couldn't tell what had caused the emotional storm. Given her determination to see this out, to deal with Tommy, he wondered if her reactions had anything to do with that at all, or if it was something else.

Something like him.

He had thought her acceptance of him was too ready, too easy. Although he had awakened the other evening smelling the remnants of her consternation and had assumed that she had been working her way through the whole thing over again. It hadn't surprised him. He had even assumed she would have to go through it a time or two again.

Just as he assumed that as soon as this mess was settled she would probably want nothing more to do with him. And he'd been very careful to make sure she could still leave when all this was over, that she wouldn't be so tied to him by desire that she couldn't make any other decision.

Maybe the worst thing of all was realizing that right now he could have cast all his scruples to the wind, could have taken her to that place that would have made her his forever whether she knew what she was getting into or not. Whether she wanted it or not. Because right now he almost sensed her slipping away and he didn't want to lose her.

She had given him an acceptance he had never thought he would know again except from his own kind. For that alone he would have wanted to keep her around.

But there was more, much more that called to him, nameless things without definition, making her more than just another tempting morsel that had crossed his path.

A deep sense of foreboding caused him concern. He turned inward, briefly, avoiding thoughts of all the danger Yvonne would face tomorrow night, given what they believed was going to happen. For a few moments, just a brief space, he allowed himself to look at places he'd shut off years ago.

And he didn't like what he found.

"Creed?"

Jude's voice called him back from the abyss.

"We need to figure out how we're going to handle this."

"I know. Luc should be here soon, right?"

"Right. But we still need a plan. And it might involve Yvonne taking a huge risk."

In an instant, Creed was on his feet, crouched and snarling. "No!"

The change was instantaneous, not a single thought preceded it. Awareness of danger to Yvonne cast him immediately into the most primitive side of his nature. Even as he caught himself in the act, he saw an expression very like understanding and knowledge on Jude's face. And shock on Yvonne's.

He tried to straighten, but his body had flooded with feral hormones, turning him into a savage hunter. Even as he struggled to return to the civilized veneer he wore most of the time, even as he realized that Jude had not threatened Yvonne himself, he needed to let out the fury that possessed him. And even in the depths of this place he tried to avoid at all costs, he was surprised by his own reaction. It had been different when Luc had kidnapped Yvonne. Then such a reaction was justified.

But just to hear Jude say she might have to put herself in danger?

The hammering in his head nearly drowned out rational thought, but not quite. Not quite, thank goodness. The wiser voice hammered at him, telling him he was overreacting.

"Creed," Jude said quietly. "We won't if we don't have to. I understand. Believe me, I understand."

If anyone did, it must be Jude, because Creed himself did not fully understand his reaction.

It seemed to have blown up out of nowhere, really.

With effort, he uncoiled himself one muscle at a time. He didn't want to look at Yvonne now, didn't want to see the horror or revulsion in her face. Didn't want to know what she really thought of him behind her politeness and kindness. Or what she must think now that she had seen this.

But then, startling him almost into another crouch, he felt a hand on his forearm. Battering down an instinctive reaction, he turned his head and saw Yvonne. She was touching him, and her face no longer reflected shock, but instead the most unexpected kindness.

"It's okay, Creed," she said softly. "Please, it's okay. No one here is going to hurt me. You know that."

Then, even though he must have looked every inch like a panther poised to spring and claw, she stepped closer and slipped her arms around him, standing within the potentially fatal circle his arms made as if she didn't fear him at all.

Her intoxicating scent reached him, filled him, carrying with it none of the fear he had sensed on her before. None of the aromas that drew him so powerfully and tried to rip away his civilized veneer.

"Shh," she said softly, and leaned into him, kissing him. The touch was a blessing.

"You should run," he said hoarsely. "While you still can, run."

"I'm not afraid of you."

"You should be."

"But I'm not."

Jude spoke, his voice an amused drawl. "Where have I heard that before?"

But Creed ignored him. He allowed Yvonne's aphrodisiacal scent to carry him to a different place, a place where he could put his arms around her gently and hold her close. He pressed his face into her hair and inhaled her as if she were salvation.

He could have stayed that way forever.

Jude eventually cleared his throat, interrupting the moment. "Sorry, people, but we have some planning to do. And Luc will be here soon."

Creed straightened, releasing Yvonne slowly, looking deep into her eyes. He read something there, though he wasn't quite sure what. It did, however, seem to him that she'd made a decision. Wondering what that decision was put him on tenterhooks, but he would just have to endure it. Now was not the time.

"How about a sheet of paper and a pencil?" Jude asked. Then he pulled out his phone and punched a number. "Garner. I need you to scope out The Far Place. Yes, tonight. I need to know if a ritual could be performed somewhere in the building, and I need to know now."

Jude disconnected before Garner could argue. Creed returned from his desk with a thin stack of paper and some pencils. "Thanks," Jude said, taking them. He placed them on the table and leaned over them.

"Okay," he said, as if momentous things hadn't just been happening around him, "here's the deal. We won't know for sure if the ritual is to be performed at the club. If Garner finds a suitable place, we can probably plan on it, but we still need to be aware that Tommy might intend to take her elsewhere."

Creed nodded, swallowing an instinctive growl. Now that the moment was nearly at hand, he was discovering just how close his vampire nature was to the surface. He didn't like it. All it did was make him unpleasantly aware that he'd been living a self-delusion for nearly a century.

There was a knock at the terrace door and he swung around quickly, seeing Luc out there. Muttering under his breath, he went to let the other vampire in.

"You started without me," Luc complained as he saw the papers on the table.

"Oh, shut the hell up," Creed said irritably. "We haven't started anything. We just got some information. You haven't missed a damn thing."

Luc arched a brow, but for once didn't say anything. Apparently his desire to get at Asmodai overrode anything else.

Jude made an impatient noise. "Let's just get to it, Luc, shall we?"

"Of course, *mon ami*."

Creed looked at Yvonne and noticed she had backed away a bit, from Luc. Her gaze retained the memory of how the other vampire had threatened her. And now she was supposed to trust him.

Creed wanted to tear something to pieces. Instead he went to stand close to Yvonne, his presence a sign of protection. Luc smiled almost scornfully.

"Okay," Jude said. "Here's how the pentagram will be laid out. And here's what we have to do. And at all costs, we can never let Yvonne out of our sight. Got it?"

Luc and Creed both nodded. Yvonne let out a shaky little sigh.

Creed reached for and clutched her hand, certain of one thing and one thing only: He would die to protect her.

Chapter 12

"Are you ready?"

Creed's question seemed to echo through Yvonne as if she had become a cavernous space inside. "Yes." As ready as she could be. Creed had spent hours reading a book Jude had given him, the Roman Ritual for Exorcism. She knew he had tucked bottles of holy water in his pockets.

She knew he carried the necklace intended to bind Asmodai. He didn't want her to touch it until the right time, for fear Asmodai might smell it around her.

"How can a necklace smell?"

"I don't know that it smells. But it's powerful and his senses are different. You understand the plan?"

She nodded. There was an unoccupied third-floor loft at the nightclub. They figured that was where the ceremony would happen.

"Okay," he said, "your cab is here. I'll walk you down."

"You're sure you can't ride with me?"

He shook his head. "But I'll never be out of eyesight, trust me."

She should have felt safe. Three vampires would be watching over her, two of them following her to the club, the third, Jude, already there to scope out the setup. Tommy wouldn't have the senses to notice them. She wished she could be sure about Asmodai.

Recalling the icy, terrifying sense of presence she'd felt in her apartment, and once in Creed's, she wasn't certain anything could protect her. She had to square her shoulders and remind herself she couldn't continue to live this way. Tommy had to be stopped. Asmodai had to be stopped.

Creed helped her into the cab and slipped money to the driver. She looked back as the taxi pulled away, but Creed had already vanished, following from the rooftops perhaps, or moving so fast she simply couldn't see him anymore.

The trip to the club seemed at once to take forever and to be over too soon. All of ten minutes in actuality, with only light traffic most of the way. When she stepped out of the cab, she was greeted by garish neon lights, crowds of young people on the sidewalk.

For an instant she froze. The idea that there was safety in numbers didn't even occur to her. She had to remind herself that as far as the vampires were concerned, there was no way she could vanish in this crowd. They could pick out her scent from a million others. A billion others. At least that's what Creed had promised her. She had to believe him.

She passed the doorman who didn't even question her age, and stepped into the raucous interior, full of noise and strobing lights that made it almost impossible to see. The loud music made the floor vibrate beneath her feet, and faces so strange they looked almost inhuman flashed at her as she looked around wondering how in the world she would find Tommy in this mob.

"Vonnie." His voice in her ear made her jump. At this point she didn't know how loud he'd shouted her name, but she knew one thing for certain. Even if she'd come here innocently, his quick discovery of her would have roused her suspicions. Waiting for Tommy had for a long time been an inescapable part of her life. Finding that he was waiting so eagerly for her only confirmed the worst: Tommy wanted something. And most likely it wasn't her.

But she knew that already. She managed a cool smile and let him take her hand even though it made her skin crawl. No longer did she admire his dark hair and blue eyes, or that smile.

"I've got a table over here," he shouted.

She nodded and let him lead her. Of course it was the table in the farthest darkest corner. *They won't lose me,* she reminded herself. They can see in the dark. They can smell me. I'm not going to get lost.

But her heart began to hammer faster than the bass beat that rattled the walls. At last she slid into the booth beside him and noticed there were already two drinks. She reached for hers, thinking only that her mouth was dry. Then so quickly that she almost missed it, she felt a hand grab her wrist. She looked down at once and saw the imprint on her skin, but no hand.

"Drugged," she heard Creed say in her ear. She jumped and looked around, but no Creed.

"What's got you so uptight?" Tommy said. "Enjoy your drink. We're just here to talk, right?"

"I'm not thirsty. And this is an impossible place to talk." God, had she just said that? Had she just suggested he take her someplace else?

"Just for a little while," he said. "There's a quieter place upstairs, but one of my buddies is using it right now. You remember Hatchet."

Of course she remembered Hatchet. He was her least favorite of Tommy's friends, and that was saying something.

"So what did you want me to talk about?" Tommy asked.

"I just…felt I left things unsaid. Undone."

"You *did* leave in a hurry." He leaned toward her, simulating contrition. Only now she knew him well enough to know when he was lying.

"I'm so sorry I screwed up. I don't know what got into me."

She couldn't help herself, and she certainly wasn't about to play the pushover regardless of what was going on. "You did what you wanted, Tommy. The way you always do."

His eyes narrowed a bit. He wasn't used to being criticized. He preferred the company of people who never took exception to anything he did or said. It kind of sickened her to remember that she'd once been one of those people, dazzled by his good looks, by the fact that he had a band and performed in clubs. In short, a mousy writer who'd been blinded by flattery and excitement.

She still had no idea why he'd noticed her, except that she was better able to pay the bills than he was. But from where she sat now, she could only marvel in disgust at her own naivety. She'd fallen prey to slick flattery. At least Creed didn't give her any of that. He was at least open and even blatant about why he wanted her: because she smelled good to him.

The thought almost elicited a laugh from her. What a change! What a different way to think about things.

"You think I'm funny?" Tommy asked. There was an edge to his voice even though she could tell he was trying to hide it.

"I'm trying to remember," she said with partial truth, "why I fell in love with you." Why she had *thought* she fell in love with him, but she omitted that part. One thing she had figured out during her final months with this man, was that whatever she had felt for him, it had never been anything as enduring as love.

No, she came closer to that with Creed. He let her see what he was, even claimed he was a monster, and that he could do terrible things. She believed he was capable of all that, yes, but unlike with Tommy, she didn't have any desire to change Creed. No, she liked him exactly the way he was, even in the terrifying moments when the predator showed, like last night.

Why? She wasn't sure. She just knew that Creed made her feel safer and more secure than Tommy ever had.

"Maybe," Tommy said after a moment, "I can remind you of what we had."

His eyes looked a little hard, and her heart squeezed with fear. The time was coming, the time she had promised herself and Creed that she was ready to face. She had to face it. Whatever this thing was that Tommy was trying to make a deal with, she knew with certainty it had to be stopped. She had felt its presence, and she could only imagine what it might be capable of if it became physical. Blood sacrifices? Deals with the devil? No, she couldn't allow this.

"What do you mean?" she asked cautiously.

"Hatchet must be done," he said. "Just come upstairs with me where it's quiet."

She hesitated, not wanting to seem too easy, afraid that if she didn't behave right she might make Tommy suspicious. "I don't know if that would be wise. You hurt me, Tommy."

"And I want to make it up to you." Wheedling again. "It's quieter upstairs. We can talk better. I've been missing you, Yvonne. Really missing you."

For an instant, just an instant, she saw the Tommy who had drawn her in the first time: exciting, intent, so very focused on her. As if she were all that mattered. And at the moment, getting her upstairs *was* probably all that mattered to him.

"I don't know..." But she allowed her voice to trail off uncertainly.

"Come on. This place is full of people. If you decide to leave, how am I going to stop you?"

He took her hand and squeezed it, and the light came into his eyes, the light that had first enchanted her, the light that said he really wanted her. Being wanted had been heady then. Being wanted by Creed ever so much more so. Tommy didn't hold a candle to Creed in any way.

She looked down, then finally nodded. It was time. She'd held back enough to be convincing.

When she lifted her gaze again, he was smiling, all ten thousand watts of a smile that made women fall into his arms. His only talent, she supposed, because music certainly wasn't one of them.

He drew her from the booth and she let him tug her gently to a back stairway. They passed no other people on their way up, but she felt a whisper of air, a sense that something had just slipped by her. Creed or Luc, she was certain. And Tommy wouldn't even notice it.

A faint smile came to her lips, even as trepidation grew stronger. Whatever waited up there might kill her. It might do terrible things to her. And a vampire army might not be enough.

"Oh, God," she said quietly, and shivered.

"It's okay," Tommy said, misinterpreting. "I'm not going to do anything to you. Have I ever hurt you physically?"

"No…no…"

"You see?" He smiled. "Just the two of us. Five minutes, ten… No more than you want. I just need to let you know how much I still care."

Yvonne's mouth was beginning to turn dry with growing fear so she didn't even bother to respond. It was all she could to try to keep her face calm enough when panic was starting to beat its icy wings.

Maybe, she told herself, they'd get upstairs and there would be absolutely nothing. Maybe she'd imagined it all. Maybe Tommy was just a worm who couldn't stand the thought that a woman had actually left him. That would certainly fit.

And she didn't believe it. She found it harder to breathe as they mounted the last stairs. Her heart hammered so loudly she could hear it herself, and thought her vampire cadre must find it deafening. Another whisper of breeze alongside her, a fleeting touch from an unseen hand. A reassurance.

She managed to draw a deep breath and climb that last stair.

They turned a corner and she froze. "Tommy?" Even though she had known, even though Jude had tried to draw a diagram, and explain last night, she still wasn't prepared for the sight that greeted her.

Tommy's grip on her tightened, pinning her to his side. "It's okay, Vonnie, we're just playing a game."

"A game?"

A game in a dark cavern of a room with five people wearing dark cloaks and hoods, standing behind five candles that marked the corners of…of a pentagram, she realized as Tommy dragged her closer.

"Tommy! You know I don't like this stuff!"

"It's just a game," he said again. "We're all friends here. Look, you know everyone."

And she did. She recognized faces of his friends, some of them in his band. Then her gaze fixed on a girl who was tied to a chair and gagged. Sheila?

"Sheila! Tommy what are you doing to her?"

"It's part of the game," Tommy said. "Sheila's having fun."

Sheila's eyes looked hazy, too hazy. Drugs, Yvonne thought. Tommy's younger sister must be drugged.

And then it hit her. Tommy was going to sacrifice his own fourteen-year-old sister. The virgin sacrifice. She tried to struggle free of Tommy's grip, but he wouldn't let go.

"It's just a game," he said again. "You'll see."

"How can you tie up your sister like that?"

"She wanted me to. She likes it."

Yvonne seriously doubted that but Sheila was so drugged she couldn't tell for certain.

"You should have had your drink," Tommy said. "You'd be enjoying yourself ever so much more."

Yvonne's instinct was to turn and run. But she couldn't do that. If ever she might have done that, it was impossible now looking at Sheila. Somehow she had to handle this so that they could bind Asmodai before anything happened to Sheila. If nothing else, that child had to get out of here in one piece.

"Oh, all right," she said irritably, jerking

away from Tommy. "Let's get this over with. Your sister ought to be home in bed."

"It's really quite simple," Tommy said. "You just stand inside the pentagram."

"That's it? That's all I have to do?"

"Absolutely. Then we'll do our little chant and it'll be all over."

She looked at him, read lies all over his face, but simply nodded. "Okay."

He smiled. "Are you getting adventurous finally?"

"I guess I am." Then, because she had to do something to make him trust her enough, she laughed, tossed her head and looked at the others. "Do you do this often?"

Some of them nodded. Some didn't make any response at all. Creepy.

"Where do I stand?" she asked Tommy, then did something she absolutely hated doing. She gave him a coquettish tilt of her head. Dog that he was, he assumed his charm still held sway over her. "Right there at the center," he said. "The very middle."

"Okay."

"Just don't scuff the lines."

Just before she crossed the outer line of the

pentagram she felt the brush of the wind again. She was not alone. She had to remember she absolutely was not alone.

All of a sudden she felt a weight in her jacket pocket. Trying to move casually, she stuck her hand into it and felt the necklace. The necklace that one of them needed to place on Asmodai. Apparently her.

Then she remembered something that gave her a breath of confidence. Asmodai had once persuaded his concubine to remove the necklace. If he could be that charming, then maybe she could pretend to be charmed enough to get close enough to hang it around his neck.

And one glance back at Sheila was enough to convince she *had* to do it. There was, for just an instant, a flicker of terror in the young girl's face.

And that flicker aroused such anger in Yvonne that it drove the last of the fear from her. Tommy was going to pay for this, and along with him whatever creature from the pit of hell had persuaded him to try this. Her fingers closed on the necklace, and she battled down an urge to say the St. Michael prayer that Creed had taught her only last night. She must do nothing to stop this until Asmodai was emerging, not until she could bind him.

She stepped into the circle.

Creed, up in a high dark corner, watched with burgeoning rage and fear. They had not planned for this. They had not dreamed that something would prevent the three of them from entering that circle.

Evidently summoning Asmodai involved powers not even Jude had encountered before, because as he looked across the cavernous space to the high beam where Jude sat, almost invisible in the shadows, he saw his concern reflected. Jude had noticed, too. At once Creed sprang and came to land silently on the beam beside Jude.

"What now?" he asked, subvocalizing at a level only a vampire could hear.

"Yvonne," Creed said. "You gave her the necklace, right?"

"I had to when I realized I couldn't enter. My God, she must be terrified. She must have realized she has to do the job."

Jude nodded.

Creed gripped his arm hard. "We have to help her."

"I'm not sure how. Keep alert. Some chance will occur."

Some chance will occur? For an instant Creed had a desire to tear Jude to shreds. Relying on chance at this point was no plan at all.

But he leaped back to his corner and watched intently, desperate to find any opportunity once that stinking demon started to emerge.

Despite himself, he looked at Yvonne's face and read her realization: it was all on her now.

He could have howled in desperation and frustration.

Yvonne became aware of whispers around her, and realized the circle of Tommy's friends was chanting some kind of mantra. Almost lost in those whispers were other faint sounds, like the wind moving down a night street: Creed, Jude and Luc. They were here, moving around, getting ready for the moment. The very weight of the necklace in her pocket, however, told her they couldn't get into the circle. The plan had been for Creed to put it on the demon who would be distracted by Yvonne as he emerged.

That plan had clearly changed. Another shudder of fear ripped through her. To buck herself up, she looked back at Sheila. She had to save that girl at any cost.

She closed her eyes, reminding herself of what she had been told to do last night. Seem to go along. Seem to be drawn to Asmodai. And now, with the necklace in her hand, apparently it fell to her to convince a demon she was attracted to him.

The whispers built around her, and the candles flickered, adding to the eeriness of the moment. No other light broke the darkness.

Sheila made a sound, struggled against her bond, then settled when Tommy bent over her, reassuring her it wouldn't be much longer. Again the haziness filled the girl's eyes.

And something approaching hatred filled Yvonne.

"Vonnie?" Tommy drew her attention back him. "Come stand over here."

"Why?"

"You've marked your presence in the center of the circle. Now you need to stand on the path."

"What path?"

He pointed to one of the lines. "Right there. Just do it, okay?"

"Okay." She managed an indifferent shrug, as if she thought this was all pretend. She moved along a chalk line until she stood between two points of the star, almost directly on the chalk line.

"That's good," Tommy said.

The chant around her was growing stronger now, and the hair began to stand up on the back of her neck. A chill trickled through her until her skin felt like ice.

The chanting seemed to hesitate for a moment, and she turned to look toward the center of the pentagram. What she saw made her heart climb into her throat. The floor there seemed to glow as if it were on fire, yet it was not burning.

Oh, my God! She could no longer deny the reality of any of this. She turned back to Tommy and saw him grinning.

"Tommy, what..."

"It's working," he said. "You'll see. But don't try to step out of the pentagram now. It's been sealed."

"What does that mean?"

"You could die," whispered a voice from behind her. She swung around again and saw a figure emerging from the firelike glow on the floor. Before her eyes, it grew until it was as tall as any man, maybe a little taller. It smiled at her. "So you are mine," it said.

Her mouth had turned as dry as the Sahara. She couldn't have formed a word to save her life. Her fingers tightened around the chain necklace in her pocket, seeking strength from it somehow, but all she wanted to do was run for her life.

The figure wavered as if it were flame itself, but did not take on completely physical form. It smiled at her, but there was no gentleness in it. And then its gaze leaped to Tommy.

"Finish it," it said.

"Yes," Tommy whispered. He turned, holding a knife she hadn't seen before and leaned over his sister. Yvonne couldn't stifle a horrified cry as he cut Sheila's wrist and blood spilled forth.

Tommy bent and pulled a cracked cup from the floor and caught his sister's blood in it. Then he turned and hurled it toward the monster in the middle of the pentagram. "A virgin's blood," he cried.

The demon let out a roar and before Yvonne's horrified gaze grew more solid. "Now her," it said, pointing at Yvonne. "Mark her for me."

Tommy turned back to his sister, dipping his fingers in blood. Yvonne felt rooted, unable to move, horror beyond words seizing her.

Then she felt the movement of air nearby, heard the barest sound of Creed's voice.

"Yvonne. Now. We can't enter…."

For what seemed like endless moments she still couldn't move, frozen with both terror and horror. And then she saw Tommy moving toward her, his bloody hand extended.

Only one way out of this now. The realization plummeted into the very soul of her being. She turned before Tommy reached her, forced a smile onto her face and said pertly, "Don't you want to mark me yourself?"

Was that her? Was that really *her?* Apparently so because the demon's gaze fastened to her, and its smile broadened. From somewhere she found the courage to walk toward it, still smiling. "I mean," she managed to say in a voice that quavered only slightly, "if you really want me, make me yours yourself."

From above, Creed watched and listened with amazement. Yvonne had figured it out. From somewhere deep within, she had found impressive reserves of strength. She had evaded Tommy's marking and now challenged the demon himself.

His entire body tightened with fear for her. The challenge she had just made might be her undoing, and there wasn't a single damn way for him to get to her to protect her.

He could have cut off his own head right then. How had they allowed this to happen? How had they failed so badly that one mortal woman now faced down the Prince of Demons all by herself?

The only thing he could promise himself was that if anything happened to Yvonne, neither Tommy nor any of his friends would survive this night. He would tear them to shreds, and he'd relish every moment of it.

The demon's head reared at Yvonne's challenge, then it laughed. That laughter seemed to free Yvonne from the last of her fear. The thought of Sheila bleeding helplessly behind her fueled her rage. And Creed had said they couldn't enter the circle. She'd heard him. Not quite last night's plan, but whatever.

She was the only one left who could do it.

She put a hand on her hip and tried to mimic women she had seen who swayed their hips in exaggerated enticement when they walked.

"You're a big guy," she said admiringly. At least she hoped it sounded admiring. "I'll bet you're powerful, too."

"I can promise you riches, travel, a life in palaces," Asmodai said. "I can place the world at your feet."

"I don't want the whole world," she said, moving closer. "But a part of it would be nice."

The demon seemed to have fixated on her now. His dark eyes never left her, even as his body grew steadily more solid, emerging from the fiery light at the center of the pentagram.

She paused. "I won't get hurt if I come too close, will I?"

"Trust me. Not a hair on your head will get hurt."

She hesitated again, pretending to be unsure,

gripping the necklace in her pocket. "So you take care of your women?"

"You can have anything you want within reason. And there'd be only one woman. You."

"Hmm. Better than Tommy."

Again the demon laughed. "Much better," he promised.

Moving now, she walked toward that creature and at the last instant yanked the necklace out. With every last ounce of courage she had, she grasped it in both hands, still concealing the Tetragrammaton in her fist.

"But we've never even kissed," she said. "What if I don't like it?"

"I promise you will." It leaned toward her, smiling, almost fully physical now.

Her time was nearly up, she realized. She leaned toward it, as if anticipating the kiss, then raised her hands as if she were going to embrace it.

It saw the necklace.

As it shrieked its rage, she managed to loop it over its head.

The roar of pain that escaped it was deafening. It tugged at the necklace but couldn't pull it off.

"Traitor!" it shrieked. It pointed a finger at Tommy. "You'll pay."

Almost as if a hurricane blew through the room, the five people at the points of the star fell over, crumbling to the floor and groaning. Three vampires were suddenly there, manhandling them, tossing them away like rag dolls.

And then Creed, beautiful wonderful Creed, gripped Tommy and lifted him right off his feet. "You," Creed growled, "should join your master."

Tommy's eyes grew huge with terror. "No! No!"

"I think so." With a snap of his arm, Creed threw Tommy into the circle and straight at the demon.

"Tell him, Yvonne. *You* command him now. Tell him."

Yvonne drew herself up, looking at the furious demon. Tell him? Then she remembered. "Go back to the pit you came from, and don't ever, ever come back."

Another roar rent the night, but it faded rapidly as the demon started shrinking back into wherever it had come from. But it was clutching Tommy as if he were a prize.

A thought occurred to Yvonne. "What if he gets Tommy to remove the necklace?"

That galvanized Creed. Now that the circle was broken, he could evidently enter it. He sped to the very center and grabbed Tommy, yanking him from the demon's clutching arms.

Asmodai gave another roar, but it was lost in the distance as he vanished. Then, with a pop, that strangely glowing space in the air vanished.

"Let's finish it," Jude said swiftly. He pulled out holy water and began to sprinkle it over everyone involved, most especially the five who had formed the circle. All the while he chanted in Latin, and the members of the circle screamed in pain at every drop of the holy water.

Luc, meanwhile, was binding Sheila's arm, his face a rictus of effort not to drink what was flowing so freely from the girl.

And then Creed's arms closed around her, holding her so tightly that she could barely breathe. "You were magnificent, Yvonne. Magnificent."

She tipped her head back, still full of adrenaline and, as a result, a bit of annoyance. "What the hell happened?" she demanded. "I wasn't supposed to do all of that. You were supposed to!"

"We couldn't cross the circle. We hadn't expected that. We simply could not cross it."

"But you just did!"

"It broke when we knocked the others away, but we didn't dare risk that until Asmodai was bound. Something about the human pentagram… Something for study later. Right now, I just want to get you out of here."

Jude interrupted. "Uh, I beg your pardon, old chap, but I need some help. I've never had to do five exorcisms at once."

"What about Sheila?" Yvonne demanded. "She needs a hospital."

"I'll take her," Luc said. "She's so drugged she'll never be sure she didn't dream it."

"And what about him?" Yvonne asked, looking down at the quivering, terrified mass that had once been the hyperconfident Tommy.

"Well," Creed said coolly, "I could rip his head off right now. I wouldn't mind in the least."

"Hmm. That sounds tempting." And for an instant it did as she glanced at Sheila. But as the adrenaline began to wear off, she knew she had to live with herself, and she knew she couldn't ask Creed to do something he would hate himself for. No matter how tempting. "I don't think so. We need a better way to deal with him."

Creed sighed. "All right. You might as well see the rest of what I can do."

As she watched in amazement, Creed lifted Tommy from the floor by the front of his shirt, holding him in one hand. Tommy's eyes nearly bugged out. Then he spoke, his voice deepening, taking on a timbre that was not quite human.

"You will forget this night. You will forget every stupid little plan you had to be a success without working for it. You will feel shame and guilt for having hurt your sister even though it was an accident."

"Yes…"

"And if I ever find out you've dabbled in the black arts again, or come anywhere near Yvonne, hell is going to look like a day at the beach. Do I make myself clear?"

"Yes…"

Then Creed tossed him to the floor. "I may

reinforce that later, but for now…" He brushed his hands against his slacks. "For now I'm done with him."

Chapter 13

They finished the exorcisms just in time to get back before daylight. Creed wrapped her in a blanket and carried her in his arms the entire way. Yvonne, despite the night's terrors, had only one wish: that he'd never put her down.

The dawn painted the eastern sky a faint pink as Yvonne and Creed slipped into his condo. Without pause, they headed for his bedroom and locked themselves within.

He hugged her tight, then tumbled onto the bed with her fully clothed. "I'm sorry," he said. "I can't stay awake."

"I know. It's okay."

But as she watched death steal over him, she felt all too wide awake herself. The night had left her feeling chilled to the bone, weakened after all the fear and adrenaline. She lay wide awake staring into the dark that preserved him, her entire worldview shattered as surely as if it were a glass she had dropped on the floor.

Things she hadn't believed in such a short time ago had become real. Too real. As she lay there, she wondered if she should try to reassemble her old life, or move on into this new world.

She could probably go back. In a few weeks or months, this would all seem like some kind of dream, a nightmare, scarcely real. And out there in the ordinary daytime world, everything would reinforce her old views. She knew that.

But that would mean giving up Creed. Wiggling around, she turned on the dim bedside lamp and looked at him. How could she wonder if she even had a choice? Maybe all she was to him was that "tempting morsel" he'd called her. Maybe he wanted nothing from her beyond a mating and a drink.

Maybe he would be glad to see her walk

away and leave him safe in the isolated tower he had built for himself away from temptations he loathed.

Maybe he loathed the urges she awoke in him. How could she know, unless she asked? And she didn't know if she dared to ask, because she wasn't sure she wanted the answer.

Anxiety ran through her every cell, and she thought she'd never be able to sleep. The night had taken a toll, however, and finally, utterly exhausted, she slipped into dreams, many of them scary, all of them filled with an aching sense of impending loss.

Creed woke first. The heat of Yvonne curled up so closely against him, her arm snug around him, held him suspended in those fiery moments of resurrection and then in a heaven only a vampire could know: human warmth.

After last night, he wouldn't have been surprised if she had not wanted to stay with him any longer. She had glimpsed his capabilities last night, could no longer even remotely think he was simply an odd kind of human. Whatever questions Luc's abduction of her hadn't answered, his own behavior had.

He'd been ready to kill for her, and he'd made no bones about it. That alone should have been enough to send her on her way.

But perhaps she was just frightened enough to need the comfort of his protection for a little while longer?

She stirred, murmuring, then he watched the amazing moments of her awakening, the soft flutter of her green eyes as she slowly emerged from slumber. And then she smiled.

"Are you all right?" he asked huskily. Last night would have made a wreck out of most people.

"I'm fine."

But he saw a shadow creep into her gaze, even as her arm tightened around him. "Yvonne?"

She bit her lower lip and dropped her gaze. At once he felt a pressure in his chest unlike anything he'd felt since he had realized that staying near his family would make him a threat. That for their sakes he had to walk away.

"Yvonne," he said again, his tone almost imploring. "Have I scared you beyond bearing?"

Her head jerked and suddenly those bright

green eyes met his again. “No! Oh, no, Creed. What made you think that?”

“I get the distinct feeling you’re not happy.”

“Oh.” A small sigh escaped her and she closed her eyes.

“Just tell me,” he demanded. “Just say it, whatever it is. Don’t go away like that.”

“I’m afraid,” she said finally, in a small voice.

He couldn’t have turned colder if the death sleep had taken him in the frozen Arctic wastes. He could barely force the words out. “Of me.”

“No! I told you it’s not that.” Her eyes seemed to spark.

“Then what? I told you I’m not a mind reader. But I smell fear and worry and sorrow all over you. Please, just tell me.”

She rolled away from him, tightening his chest even more with her rejection. God, how had he been such a fool as to come to care to this degree? He knew better than to think many mortals could tolerate his kind except for the sexual thrills he had refused to fully give her.

Now he saw rejection in the way she pulled from him and gave him her back. He squeezed his eyes shut for a moment, and knew that he had fallen into that place every vampire tried to avoid: he had claimed her. Without any assurance whatever, despite his efforts to avoid it, he had claimed her. And he had claimed her while ensuring that she was still free to leave him.

His future, once nearly endless and unwanted, suddenly shrank to a few moments or hours. When she left he'd have two choices: to stalk her endlessly, or to seek mercy. And he knew which option he would choose. Pain seared him all the way to whatever soul he had left.

She sat up, her back still toward him. "This is embarrassing," she said, her voice sounding both thick and weak. "Creed…"

"Yes?" He steeled himself to hear what she really thought of him, and plenty of ugly words sprang to his mind. He knew them well because he'd often applied them to himself.

"Creed, I'm afraid of losing you!"

The words burst from her in a rush, so fast he wasn't sure he heard her correctly. "Losing me?" he repeated, uncertain.

"Yes. I know it's too fast, I know you keep

saying I don't appreciate what you are. That I don't really understand. Maybe I don't. But this week… Creed, am I just a woman who smells good to you? Or am I more?"

Never had he felt quite as torn as he did in that instant. Part of him wanted to leap for joy at what she was suggesting. Another part of him insisted that if he really cared for her, he would send her away, protecting her from his unnatural existence.

But in the end, the strength of his yearning outweighed his conscience. This once he didn't have the strength of will to deny himself what had become essential to his life. "You're more to me than you can possibly know."

Slowly she turned until she looked at him over her shoulder. "Really?"

"Really. I would have died for you last night if I had needed to. I would have killed for you. You are more important to me than I am."

Her face brightened, and she turned toward him, sitting cross-legged. He wished she would come closer, but apparently she wasn't ready to yet.

"I hope you never have to do either of those things for me," she said with a gravity that touched him. Then an impish smile tipped the corners of her mouth. "But it's kind of nice to know you would."

He felt a smile begin to dance around his own lips. "Yvonne, I've tried. I've tried to make it clear to you what I am and how I live. I've tried to keep no secrets. Do you believe me when I tell you I'm by nature a predator?"

She tipped her head. "Yes. I've always believed lions and tigers were beautiful. I've thought this over more than once. I've wondered if I was losing my mind. Then I realized something."

"What's that?"

"We are what we are. And I love you, even the parts of you you're not so proud of. And I love you all the more because you have to fight yourself so hard to do what you believe is right."

A shell that encased his heart, one that was nearly a century old, cracked wide open. He held out his arms and she came to him readily, willingly, as hungry for him as he was for her.

This time he held nothing back from her. He couldn't any longer. He ripped the clothes from them both, tearing fabric, popping buttons, bringing her into the most basic part of him. She came willingly, unafraid, giving her tender flesh to him with utter trust.

He painted fire all over her with his hands and mouth. He let her touch him in ways he hadn't permitted to anyone in forever. And then he slipped into her, claiming her as a man claims a woman.

Finally, he claimed her as a vampire claims his mate, sinking his teeth into her, drinking from her deeply, reveling in her cries of ecstasy as he took her with him to that borderland between death and life.

"I love you," he growled. "And you're mine. Claimed."

Her eyelids fluttered. "Claimed?"

"Forever. I'll never let you go. You know what that means." For an instant he knew terror that the idea of being claimed might repel her.

"Claimed," she repeated as if she savored the word. Then in the same instant, a tear leaked from one eye and a smile lifted her face. "I've never wanted anything more than I want to be yours. Always." She wrapped herself tightly around him. "I love you. Make me like you,

Creed. I want to be like you. I want to be with you forever."

"No," he whispered, forcing himself to a moment of sanity even as heaven called to him. "Later. Much later. Wait. For my sake. I need to be sure you're sure."

Their eyes met, and he saw his answer there. She would wait, but not too long.

He could deal with that. Because now there was ample time for them both.

Then he closed his eyes, buried his fangs in her tender breast, and took her with him to that place only vampires could go, hearts beating as one, bodies feeling as one.

Claimed. Forever.

* * * * *

Special Offers

Every month we put together collections and longer reads written by your favourite authors.

Here are some of next month's highlights—and don't miss our fabulous discount online!

On sale 18th May

On sale 1st June

On sale 1st June

Find out more at
www.millsandboon.co.uk/specialreleases

Visit us Online

0512/ST/MB375